Made In Paradise

Made In Paradise

A Family Forever Series, Book 2

Donna Fasano

Find the author:

Facebook – Facebook.com/DonnaFasanoAuthor

Twitter – Twitter.com/DonnaFaz

Pinterest – Pinterest.com/DonnaFaz

Instagram – Instagram.com/Donna_Fasano

Contents

Introduction

A Secret Made in Paradise...

Her child is alive! For ten years Amber has believed her child was lost to her forever. Then an unexpected inheritance leads the lovely doctor back home... to the man she's always loved. There she discovers her beloved Jon is a bachelor father, and the little girl he is raising is their daughter!

Jon has vowed to protect and cherish his child, yet he opens their lives to let Amber in. But this dedicated father is no longer the young lover Amber remembers. Can she uncover the tender man she has never forgotten, and convince him to take a chance on their newly formed family, and their own true love?

Prologue

She simply could not put off this chore any longer. Amber Holloway stood at the threshold of her father's bedroom door. The late-afternoon sun slanted golden through the window, casting streaks of light across the worn, brown rug. Absently Amber worried her bottom lip between her teeth and went inside.

The air still held a whispery trace of familiar spicy aftershave. Barely noticeable after all these weeks, the scent offered her a vague sense of comfort as she inhaled it deeply into her lungs, yet her heart pinched in her chest with painful longing.

The dark-stained pine of the bed's footboard was scarred and dull with age, the mattress sagging in the middle. Amber smiled at the memory of her father allowing her an occasional, albeit short, bed-jumping session when she'd been a little girl. She grazed her fingertips lightly across the cotton spread.

Two small steps had her standing in front of his bureau, and without even picking up the pipe that rested there, Amber detected the faint aroma of tobacco. The rich fragrance kindled feelings of deep love and total security the likes of which she would never again experience.

"Daddy," Amber whispered to the empty room. Her eyes stung as unexpected tears shattered her sight into fragments of glittering light. "Oh, how I miss you."

A month had passed since Harry Holloway's funeral. For weeks Amber had found one excuse after another to keep from sorting through his belongings, packing up his clothes, cleaning out his bedroom.

But the chill of fall was in the air and close on its heels would be winter. She was certain there was someone in need of warm clothing. Her father's gray wool overcoat might be a bit frayed at the cuffs, but it would certainly keep someone toasty when the temperatures dipped low. And his olive mackintosh was just as rain repellent as ever. There were several suits. Trousers and a sport coat or two. Dress shirts and ties. Not to mention shoes. Three pairs to be exact, all in good condition, seeing as how her father worked all his life in one shoe repair shop or another. It would be a sin to let such serviceable clothing hang in the closet and sit in the drawers, unused.

Amber dashed a tear trail from her cheek with the back of her hand. "This simply has to be done," she told herself, giving the words an insistent inflection. "*Today.*"

The topmost bureau drawer slid open and Amber dived into it with both hands, scooping out paired socks that had been rolled into balls and stragglers that had no mate but that her father hadn't been able to get rid of. There were neatly folded handkerchiefs, at least a dozen of them, one of which her dad slid into his back pocket every day. Harry Holloway would never have been caught without his trusty handkerchief. One never knew when one's glasses would need a good cleaning, or a park bench brushed off, or a little girl's nose wiped...

Again, Amber felt an achy spasm shoot through her chest.

"We're thick as thieves, me and you, Amber

girl." She could almost hear his soft, gentle voice as he'd described their close and loving relationship. Her dad had been an emotional man. Yes, he had been.

She sniffed back another tear. "Stop, darn it," she chastised herself aloud.

Aggravated with herself, Amber pulled the second drawer completely free and dumped its contents onto the bed. V-necked T-shirts and cotton boxers tumbled into a pile. The third drawer held polo shirts and sweaters. One shabby-looking sweatshirt caught her eye and she picked it up. The pilled fabric was soft against her cheek and she remembered this was her father's favorite. The one he wore to work around the house. She set it aside. A cherished keepsake.

She found several pairs of shorts in the fourth drawer, and as she tossed them into the pile, she noticed they were threadbare in places. How few of them there were wasn't lost on her, either. Amber had been aware that her father had gone without for her. Boy, had she been aware.

He'd worked so hard. Had sacrificed so much. Just so she could earn the title of Dr. Amber Holloway. His greatest wish had been to provide her with a college and medical school education free from the strangling claws of bank loans. For several years he'd been successful, paying for her tuition and books with his meager salary, but not without a great deal of personal sacrifice. Because of Amber, Harry Holloway never took a vacation, never bought a new car, and just simply made do with what he had or could acquire secondhand.

Not wanting the pile of her father's clothing to become so large it rolled to the floor, she stopped clearing out drawers and began to lovingly tuck the clothing into a large plastic bag.

Her protests against all his sacrifice had fallen on deaf ears. Harry hadn't allowed Amber to work anything more than a part-time job all through her college years.

But as the tuition increased, and his salary hadn't, Harry was forced to allow Amber to seek out student loans through the University of Connecticut; however, he'd done everything he could to keep those debts to a minimum.

Amber had just finished her medical residency and had accepted a partnership in a large family practice. Her loans were almost miniscule compared to some of her graduating peers, and she was in a much better position than they would be for years to come. All due to her father's ceaseless efforts to pay the tuition bills, all due to his endless determination to set aside his own needs to provide for those of his daughter.

Once the bed was clear, she turned back to the bureau and bent to pull out the final drawer. A thought struck her with such startling suddenness that her spine straightened almost of its own accord, and she rested her hand on the bureau top.

With the smell of her father's pipe tobacco wafting around her, she realized that with all his making do, with all his self-sacrifice, he'd never once over the years made her feel the least bit guilty. He'd never made one comment to make her feel beholden. Never said a word meant to incite her need to feel obligated or indebted to him. He'd never once brought up her mistakes of the past. He'd simply given to her. He'd simply loved her. Unselfishly. Unconditionally.

He'd been such a kind, caring, *loving* parent.

With a sigh, Amber returned to the task at hand. She tugged the final, bottommost drawer from its slot and twisted toward the bed. Sweatpants and heavy work trousers fell out along with something that made a heavy *clunk* as it bounced onto the mattress.

Curiosity knitted her brow as she brushed aside

one leg of a pair of navy sweatpants to see the object more clearly.

It was a box. A tin box. A tad smaller than a shoe box. The blue paint had chipped away in several places, allowing rust to eat at the metal.

The edge of the mattress depressed as Amber sat down. She picked up the box, acutely aware of the coolness of its surface. The latch caught, and for a moment she thought the box was locked. But the latch finally gave, and the lid sprang free.

Envelopes, a tight bundle of them, were crammed in the tight space. A rubber band secured them together. These weren't regular white letter envelopes. They looked official. No, they looked like oversize, tan *business* envelopes. And they were unopened. Amber had to strain to pry them out of the cramped space. There looked to be over a hundred of them. However, before she was able to examine them too closely, her attention was caught by the small book resting in the bottom of the box. The tiny book's rough, black cover was reminiscent of the old register books banks gave out before the age of computerized accounts. Utter bewilderment had her head shaking back and forth as she wondered what in the world she'd discovered.

After setting the envelopes aside, Amber picked up the bankbook, turned it over and her mouth opened in surprise, but no sound came forth.

Weston Savings And Loan, Pine Meadow, N.J.

Walloped with an overwhelming wave of weakness, she was relieved to be sitting because her whole body felt suddenly shaky. That name. Weston. It hadn't been mentioned between her and her father in many years.

Seldom did Amber allow herself to even think it, because doing so only stirred up memories. Haunting memories of a love she'd felt so strongly the mere thought of it was enough to swallow her whole. But when she did indulge herself, when she did permit herself to get lost in remembering, she did so only in the very deepest part of the night, when there was no chance of her reminiscence being discovered.

However, the Weston name also conjured in her an ache. A terrible anguish caused by a loss so complete it had left a hole in her life that would never be filled.

With well-practiced determination, she shoved the tormenting memory aside. It was either that, or risk getting completely caught up in the past.

She focused on the tin box instead. What did

it mean, this old account book? These unopened bank statements?

Her fingers trembled as she cracked open the spine of the small black book. The balance scrawled on the yellowed page made her gasp aloud.

Chapter One

"Sounds like Ol' Lady Warrington let that hairy rat she calls a dog crawl up into this engine."

Jon Weston listened intently to the rough idle of the sweet, old Cadillac, his eyes riveted to the running engine.

"The first thing we need to do," he said over the engine noise, "is pop off the distributor cap. Make sure it's clean. No cracks."

His daughter knew this already, he was sure. She was nearly ten years old now, and she'd been working on cars with him since she was a babe in diapers. But it never hurt to reiterate.

"Hand me a flathead screwdriver, Syd."

The tool that was slapped into his palm didn't have a flat, smooth head, but the crisscrossed one of a Phillips. He grinned. He had Sydney now. This mistake was downright silly and deserved at least an hour's worth of teasing. And he'd gladly oblige.

"You're in for it now," he said. But when he swung around expecting to see Sydney, he came face-to-face with his stem-eyed mother.

When she offered him no greeting, he said, "Hi, Ma. How are you?"

"First of all," she told him, "I take offense for poor Edith Warrington. She is *not* an old lady..."

"Aww, now." He grinned, hoping to soften her obvious disapproval. "I didn't mean any harm."

"*And* Corky is a lovely little long-haired terrier," she went on. "Not 'a hairy rat.' Edith is a wonderful friend. And she loves that dog like a baby. If she ever heard you talk like that—"

"She's not going to hear me talk like that, Ma," Jon assured his mother.

"The only reason Edith patronizes your shop—" her gaze skirted loathsomely around the cluttered bay "—is because you are my son, and—"

"I know, Ma." Jon's smile dissolved. His mother had a way of making that happen quite often. "And I appreciate the business your name brings me."

"It's your name, too."

If only you'd do something with it. Her blatant

motherly advice echoed unspoken in the air. He chose to ignore it.

Helen Weston tipped up her chin. And Jon got the distinct impression that, now that she'd had her say, the subject was closed. He sighed.

"So what brings you out this afternoon?" he asked. He watched his mother glance over her shoulder at her granddaughter who sat behind the steering wheel of Edith Warrington's old Caddy.

She turned back to face him. "Why isn't missy there in school?"

"Her name's Sydney, Ma," he said quietly.

"Look at her," Helen continued. "She's filthy. Her hair's a mess. Her fingernails are greasy. And she's—"

"Ma." His voice was clipped just enough to make her stop. "Let's talk about this in my office." Giving his daughter a quick glance, he said, "Cut the engine, hon. I'll be right back."

He stalked off toward the side door leading to his office, making every effort to dampen the burning embers of his anger.

Jon was well aware of the fact that he was his mother's worst and only disappointment. That he was no comparison to his brother and sister, both shining examples of the education, polish, and success that Weston money could buy. And because he knew all these things, took full responsibility for them, he tried hard to be patient with her.

Flipping on the overhead light, Jon felt a self-conscious tweak as he looked around at the shabby furniture. The sorry excuse he called a desk was beat-up, the heavy gray metal dented and scratched. The couch was propped up on one corner by a red brick. And the leather seat of his desk chair was cracked in several places.

Funny how he never seemed to notice how neglected his surroundings were until his mother came to visit. Which, thankfully, was only on rare occasions.

"Have a seat," he told her, rounding his desk and easing himself down onto his chair.

She eyed the couch distastefully. "I don't mind standing, thank you."

"Suit yourself." He snatched up a pen from the desktop, squeezing it between his thumb and index finger. "Sydney had a headache this morning," he explained. "She came to work with me and took a nap in my office. She woke up feeling better, so she was helping me out in the shop."

"Well, when she woke up feeling better," his

mother stated, "you should have taken her to school."

"Ma—" Jon's shoulder sagged with the effort of this justification, but he was so used to this kind of interrogation that he barely noticed. "It's after two o'clock. She'd have been in school an hour." Then a thought occurred to him. "How did you know Sydney wasn't in school today?"

Helen Weston's lips pursed for an instant. Then she said, "If you must know, I asked the school secretary to call me if Sydney was absent."

Patience, Jon reminded himself. He asked softly, "Why would you do a thing like that?"

"Jon, this is a new school year. Sydney *must* start off on the right foot." She shifted the position of the purse handle that hung on her forearm. "I don't know why you won't allow me to send the child to boarding school. I sent you to boarding school." She paused, as if she had second thoughts about the statement, eyeing him pointedly.

And just look what you did with the education I provided for you.

His mother's accusation couldn't have been clearer if she'd said it out loud.

Then she added, "As well as your brother and sister,"

"Public school is fine for Sydney, Ma," he told her. "All Sydney's friends attend the school here in Pine Meadow. She'd be miserable if she had to go to a new school. She's getting a fine education right where she is."

He didn't want his daughter feeling as lonely and out of place as he had felt as a youngster being shipped off to boarding school. He had hated every moment he'd been away from Pine Meadow and his friends and family. However, he'd bent to his mother's will because as a child he'd had no other choice. Until high school, anyway, when he'd discovered that a threatened expulsion due to fist fighting with his classmates was the perfect way to force her to let him attend school here at home.

"Yes," his mother said, "and she's getting that education along with every piece of riffraff Pine Meadow has to offer."

"You know my views on that subject," Jon said wearily. "Sydney's going to be dealing with all kinds of people as an adult. Black, white, yellow, brown, rich, and poor. It'll do her good to learn to get along with everyone while she's a kid."

"Huh, maybe." Helen Weston was obviously unconvinced. Then her eyes lit with a new attack. "But boarding school would get her away from this place. And it's this grease pit I most want to get her away from. She should be taking piano lessons, or ballet lessons. She should be reading *Black Beauty* and *Little Women*. That child should be wearing lacy dresses and patent leather shoes."

She stopped suddenly, hesitating long enough to take a deep breath, gather her frayed wits.

"Jon, that child is soon going to be ten years old. She's a young lady now. She shouldn't be tinkering underneath the hood of a car, her hands filthy with grease. This... this *mechanic shop*—" she said the two words as if they were knives stabbing her in the eyes "—isn't any place for a young lady. It isn't right that you're allowing Sydney to follow you around like some oily little monkey whose only goal in life is to hand her father a screwdriver or a pocket wrench."

Up until now, he'd been resting his chin on his fist. But the moment his mother had called his daughter a greasy primate, he'd had to clamp his fingers over his mouth, his thumb planted firmly under his jaw to keep from growling at her to get the hell out of his office, out of his shop.

She's only trying to help, he chanted in his head. *She only wants what's best for her granddaughter.*

"I think you mean socket wrench," he muttered.

His mother only offered him a deadpan stare.

He glanced out the window that separated his office from the three work bays that made up the shop. Sydney had her head stuck under the hood of the car parked in the first bay. The bill of her baseball cap was twisted to the back of her head. Her elbows and knees were nut brown with grime, her denim shorts and cotton top smeared and grubby as well. His heart hitched in his chest. That little girl was his whole life. His whole world.

"That child needs some feminine influence," Helen said. "And if she doesn't get it soon, it's going to be too late. You mark my words."

Too late for what? Jon was too preoccupied to ask. He was too busy wondering if his mother might be right. Was he doing Sydney wrong by allowing her to spend time at the shop? Should he be chauffeuring her around to piano lessons and ballet recitals rather than teaching her how to read on-board diagnostics? How to change an engine's spark plugs and fuel filter?

"I think you ought to let Sydney move in with me," Helen said.

His knee-jerk reaction was to say, "No way." But the response fell on deaf ears.

"I can teach her to be a proper young lady, Jon,"

his mother argued. "You do want her to grow up into a woman who can hold her head up in this town, don't you? You do want her to be proud of who she is? Do you think that's going to happen when she spends most of her life—" she looked around again, disdain evident in every muscle of her face "—hanging around *Jon's Auto Repair?*"

Usually he wasn't at all fazed by the disgust his mother showed when she spoke the name of his business. Usually he allowed her disappointment in him to roll off him like water off a rain slicker. Usually. But today it struck him—like a forceful, unexpected poke in the gut with a tire iron.

"You think about it," his mother said. "And when you do, I want you to consider long and hard what's best for Sydney. Not what's best for you."

She opened the door of his office then, and carefully picked her way through the dirty clutter of car parts toward the big open door of the garage bay, taking care not to allow the hem of her yellow dress to become soiled. Helen Weston called a curt goodbye to her granddaughter and then disappeared from his view.

Almost immediately, Sydney was standing in the threshold of his office. "You okay, Dad?"

He nodded. "Sure, hon," he told her. "Give me a few minutes, okay?"

She shot him a quick, commiserating smile and then went back to fiddling with the Caddy's engine.

Jon sat at his desk for a long time, studying her. Tendrils of wavy red hair escaped from under the cap on her head. Concentration creased her brow as she searched in the large metal box for some tool or other. The love he felt for that little girl out there was so great it actually made his chest ache. And he found it more than a little worrisome to think that letting her hang out here at the shop with him might be harming her in some way.

Okay, he thought, so we have a problem. His daughter's femininity needed a little... fine-tuning. Hell, he told himself, tell the truth; Syd's feminine side needed a complete overhaul!

As much as he hated to admit it, his mother was probably right. Sydney should be reading great works of literature. She should be involved in culturally enriching activities. And there couldn't possibly be a less likely place for a little girl to find polish and refinement than an auto repair shop.

He stroked his chin over and over between his index finger and thumb as his mind churned.

Boarding school was out of the question in his mind. But was the solution packing Sydney off to live in Weston House with his mother?

"Over my dead body," he whispered too low for anyone but himself to hear.

* * *

Pine Meadow certainly hadn't changed much in the ten years she'd been away, Amber mused as she drove through town. Certainly, the strip mall on the main thoroughfare was new, or at least new to her, as the shops had looked well established when she'd passed by them. But the First Methodist Church looked the same as ever. As did the supermarket on the corner of Main and North Streets. And the fact that the billboard hovering over the double doors of the Main Street Theater advertised Hollywood's hottest movie let her know the cinema was still going strong. Amber had spent many a Saturday afternoon in the cool, dark recesses of that movie house while her father was busy at his shop. And then as a teen, her theater visits changed to Saturday *nights*. When she'd sneaked out on dates with Jon Weston.

His name whispered across her mind, across her

thoughts, sending shivers skittering across her skin.

Lord, how she had loved that boy. And the things she'd learned from him...

Tenderness. Commitment. Affection. Passion.

The closeness and devotion they had shared rivaled even that between Shakespeare's Romeo and Juliet.

Amber's mouth quirked at one corner. The melodramatic manner in which she thought of her relationship with Jon was inevitable, entirely natural, she guessed, seeing as how she'd been so young when they'd been a couple. Her smile faded, though, because along with tender passion, he'd taught her other things as well.

Pain. And guilt. And anger.

The awful names he'd called her had the flush of humiliation rushing to her face even after all this time. It was so sad that the three wonderful years they spent together were marred forever by that hostile, accusation-filled fight they'd had. The fight that had her finally agreeing to leave Pine Meadow with her father. The hateful words Jon had used as weapons to assault her had been a devastating turning point in her life. Without them, without hearing Jon's opinion of her face-to-face, she'd have never left New Jersey. She'd have never run away from the young man who had captured her heart so completely. No matter the threats from his well-respected and wealthy family. No matter the consequences.

Braking for a red light, she forced herself to rise from the foggy haze of her memories. She'd automatically switched on her left turn signal, and as she waited for the traffic light to change, she realized she was staring at the red brick building that had always been the home of Weston Savings and Loan.

Fear welled up inside her seemingly out of nowhere. A fear so pure, so unadulterated, it had her heart pounding, her blood whooshing in her eardrums. It didn't matter a whit that the panic threatening to overwhelm her was irrational. The fact that Helen Weston, or the rest of the Weston clan, could no longer hurt her was too logical a thought; besides, it was buried under about a dump truck load of frantic insanity that had perspiration prickling her underarms and her brain screaming at her to get the hell out of this town, get the hell away from the prejudice of the judgmental Westons. Such thinking caused nothing but heartache, humiliation, and hurt for people like herself.

She'd worked so hard not to obsess about the account book she'd found among her father's possessions. But now questions and assumptions swam in her head until she thought she'd surely drown in them.

Had her father accepted some kind of payoff from Helen Weston? There really was no other explanation that Amber could come up with. Had they really been paid to leave Pine Meadow? She shook her head, thinking the only possible answer to that was yes. And all this time Amber had been under the impression she and her father had left town of their own free will, with their chins held high, their pride intact. But it seemed their exodus had been under a whole different set of circumstances entirely. But if what she surmised was true, why hadn't her father used that money when the two of them had been in such need of it over the years? The interest had accrued on that account, and not one dime had ever been withdrawn. That didn't seem to make sense, and it was that part of the situation that had her curious for answers. It was that part of the situation that had compelled Amber to take a leave of absence from her new practice and travel to Pine Meadow.

She had to admit, there was one question that haunted her more than any other. Had Jon been aware of the payoff?

A horn blared behind her and she stomped her foot on the gas pedal, desperate to get away from the bank and all the mocking questions it conjured. Her tires screeched a complaint as she took the turn much too quickly. Another turn had her heading toward Pine Meadow's east end. The "Bowers," as the area had been known years ago. The wrong side of the tracks. The bad part of town. *Her* part of town.

She slowed the car and gulped in several deep breaths in an effort to calm her troubled mind. Being back in her neck of the woods, seeing her old haunts, somehow comforted her. And she focused all her attention on them, the narrow streets and close-packed businesses soothing her frazzled nerves.

Home. The businesses in the Bowers had been mostly small, family-owned enterprises that struggled from month to month to remain open. These people had known no other way of life. Had no other means to eke out a living. And from the looks of things, that hadn't changed.

She turned down Cox Avenue and slowed down when she came to the building her father used to rent as his shoe repair shop. The main floor of the small building housed a coffee shop now. And seeing the frilly, faded yellow curtains hanging in the two upstairs windows, she surmised that someone lived in the tiny one bedroom apartment where she had been raised.

Heaving a forlorn sigh, she continued driving down the street. She'd played hopscotch on this sidewalk as a little girl. Jumped rope with her friends. Amber wrapped herself in the warm blanket-like memory of the love and security she'd felt as a child. Looking both ways at the four-way stop, that's when she saw it.

Jon's Auto Repair.

The small, metal placard advertising Body Work dangled from below the Auto Repair sign, as if it had been added on. A second thought.

Could it be...?

"No," came her verbal reply. Jon Weston's favorite hobby might have been working on cars, but he'd made it clear that he was going into his family's banking business. Abundantly clear.

Besides, a Weston would never be caught dead opening a business in the Bowers.

Still, her eyes remained glued to that sign. It seemed to call out to her. Relentless. Enticing. Like a glass of cool water to someone dying of thirst.

"Hey, there!"

Amber's gaze whipped around to see an elderly lady standing on the corner.

"You lost?" she asked.

"Oh, no," Amber told her. "I grew up around here. Lived overtop the coffee shop a couple of blocks back. My dad had a shoe repair shop there."

"Well, now." The woman smiled. "I don't remember the shop being anything other than a coffeehouse. But I've only lived here for seven years. Ever since I had to move in with my daughter and her husband." Her smile widened. "Welcome home."

"Thanks." Amber's tone was vague as her eyes were inexorably drawn back to the auto repair shop. Then she found herself saying, "Things haven't changed too much." She paused. "But I see there are a few new businesses in the Bowers..."

The hesitation had been purposeful. Amber hoped the woman would reveal some information regarding the garage across the street.

The woman chuckled. "The city council has tried every way possible to get people to stop calling this place the Bowers. They started a campaign a few years back. Wanted us to call this part of town East Meadows. That fell flat. People use what they know, I guess. And this place will always be the Bowers, won't it?"

"I guess," Amber said, her gaze never leaving the building she'd hoped to learn more about.

Finally the woman seemed to perceive her interest "You know Jon Weston?"

After several moments Amber was able to get her tongue to work. "I did. Once. A long time ago." The curt sentences sounded rough and eroded to her own ears.

"That Jon fought his family, the city council, and a whole army of other people when he wanted to open his garage over here."

By *over here*, Amber knew she meant in this less reputable part of town.

Movement caught her eye, and then she saw him. He stood in the large open doorway of the first bay, directing as someone backed a large car out of the garage. Amber felt every nerve ending in her body come alive, alert.

Jon Weston. In the flesh. She'd know the set of

those wide, muscular shoulders anywhere, recognize the tilt of that chin. That was the man who had stolen her heart. The man who had taught her what love between two people was all about. However, he was also the man who had crushed her spirit, hurt her like no one else ever had. The man who had fathered her stillborn baby girl. Her gaze never wavered from his fine form as her mind churned with all these bits from the past.

"You know," the woman said to her, "seeing as how you knew Jon and all, and seeing as how you're in the neighborhood, you ought to stop in over there and say hello."

Amber's voice actually quivered as she answered, "I think I'll do that."

Chapter Two

The broad expanse of his chest made the navy, run-of-the-mill uniform shirt look not quite so run-of-the-mill. The rolled-up sleeves revealed powerful, tanned hands and forearms, the open collar, a corded neck that invited a woman's lips to explore.

Amber started with a tiny twitch, her eyes widening. Where had *that* thought come from?

From the deepest depths of your memory, came a silent answer. *That most sensuous of places that Jon had awakened when you were just seventeen.*

Well, she decided, such thoughts would simply have to go straight back to wherever they came from, and she'd have to shut the door on them. *Lock* the door on them. And toss away the key.

After checking the street traffic one more time,

she inched across the intersection and then steered toward the asphalt parking lot of the garage.

She stopped the car, its engine idling softly. "Are you out of your mind?" she whispered to herself. "What are you doing?"

Did she really believe Jon would want to see her after all this time? After all the mean words they had hurled at each other?

But that seemed like a lifetime ago. They were both adults now, weren't they?

She cringed at the question, remembering how very grown-up she'd thought she'd been at seventeen. Seventeen and pregnant.

Again, she brushed her memories of the past aside, turning the key to cut the engine. There were questions that needed answers. She really didn't care one way or the other if Jon would want to see her. He was going to see her.

Amber got out of her car, but it was the sound of her door closing that had him looking her way. He called out for the driver of the big, white Cadillac to stop, and the car halted with a slight jerk.

His dark head tilted the tiniest bit and those deep green eyes of his narrowed, a frown creasing his brow.

She stopped about ten feet from him. A buffer zone of sorts.

"Hello, Jon," she said, reaching up and pulling off her sunglasses.

His gaze widened just a fraction with recognition when she spoke, almost as though he'd known who she was, but refused to believe it until she actually addressed him. A dozen wild gypsies stomped out a boisterous jig on her nerves as she awaited his response.

* * *

Ho-ly hell! Amber. Amber Holloway. How she'd changed!

The teenage girl who had knocked him out of his high-top basketball sneakers all those years ago had been rail-thin, the sprinkling of freckles across her nose and cheeks irresistible to him then.

Apparently the coltish Amber had grown up. Her girlish figure had filled out with the kind of womanly curves that fueled a man's dreams when he was asleep and vulnerable. And not a single freckle could be found on her pale-as-moonlight complexion. Her manicured nails told him she'd broken the childish proclivity of nibbling on them when she was worried. Remembering how she'd lamented, again and again, what she'd thought was an unbreakable habit, he nearly smiled. Nearly. But he successfully reined it in.

But one thing about her hadn't changed. Her eyes. Brown as rich, dark chocolate, and just as luscious.

That gaze alone was enough to have his libido churning to life way down low in his gut. But put together the whole package, the angelic face, the bewitching curves, and no man was safe against a gnawing hunger that had nothing to do with food. The grown-up Amber Holloway would tweak the sexual appetite of any man.

Reaching into his back pocket with as much nonchalance as he could muster, he pulled out an oily old rag. He wiped at the grease on his forearm and said, "Well, well, well."

Immediately he bit down on a silent groan. For years he'd practiced what he'd say if Amber were ever to show up in his life again. He'd filled a multitude of aching, need-filled nights imagining this moment, coming up with witty, double entendres meant to show her how great he was doing without her and make her regret leaving Pine Meadow, leaving him. But what had just come out of his mouth couldn't have sounded more lame.

Absently he stuffed the rag into his back pocket. "Look what just blew in with the wind."

Oh, Lord. He was going from bad to worse.

It must be this damned surge of testosterone. The rush of hormones was hogging his body's blood flow, making it impossible for his brain, or his tongue, to function properly.

Enough! the logical part of his mind cut in like a razor-edged knife. Why the hell are you lusting after this woman? Isn't she the one who left you all alone? Isn't she the one who sent Sydney to you with an attitude so casual, so blasé, it seemed to say she thought their child was like some stray mutt that needed tending?

His jaw clenched tight. Good. Anger. Strong enough to sink his teeth into. Strong enough to suffocate the desire burning a hole deep in his belly.

Like a flurry of sharp blows to his chin, memories bombarded him. Sydney, crying with diaper rash, and he, a new father who knew zip about a cure. Sydney, sick and weepy with a high fever. Sydney, demanding attention when he was nothing but dog tired after a long day at work.

Excellent, he thought. He wanted to recall all the bad experiences he'd had as a single father. He urged those fearful, nerve-racking, irritating memories forward, in fact. They would be the perfect stones and mortar to build himself a sturdy wall of defense against the woman standing in front of him.

"So—" he heard the clipped edge in his tone and liked it, latched onto it, actually, as if it was some kind of weapon with the ability to protect him "—you've finally come to see how your little puppy dog has fared after all these years."

A light autumn breeze blew a few wayward strands of her glorious red hair into her face and she shoved them back with her free hand, her long nails combing through the tresses with one smooth stroke. Only when her face was free from obstruction did he see the bewilderment knitting her brow, clouding those gorgeous mahogany eyes.

"My little..."

Her words faded as she stopped to moisten her lips, and the sight of her delicate pink tongue sent his heart hammering his ribs like the pistons of a prime, ass-kicking, 500-horse-power engine. Time had turned her into a beautiful and elegant swan.

Not that she'd been an ugly duckling as a teen.

No stretch of the imagination could have him saying that. Hell, she'd been cute as a damn kitten. He was reminded just how cute she'd been every time he looked at Sydney—Amber's spitting image. But the years that had passed had made the woman in front of him far more than merely attractive. She was a radiant, dazzling diamond.

Suddenly he blinked. Was that pain he read in her gaze? What the hell did she have to feel hurt about?

"I never thought of you like that, Jon," she said softly. "I never did."

Rage flashed red before his eyes like leaping flames.

"Me?" he snarled. "I'm not talking about me."

The frown in her brow bit deeper, but he was so infuriated he couldn't be bothered giving it a second thought.

"I'm talking about the little stray you so heartlessly sent back to me," he ranted on quietly. "The runt you thought was so useless you didn't even give her a name before you got rid of her."

"I'm—"

Jon watched her head shake, her hand raise to splay at the base of her throat.

"I, ah, I don't under—"

Sydney chose that very moment to shut off the engine, open the heavy door of the Caddy and get out of the car. Glancing back over his shoulder, he was grateful to see that the car's windows had been closed. Maybe the noise of the idling engine had kept his daughter from hearing what he'd said. Lord, he hoped so. The last thing he wanted was for Sydney's self-esteem to be injured by thinking she hadn't been wanted. Although that was the fact of the matter—at least from Amber's side of things.

"Daa-aad." Sydney drew out the word as only an eager, impatient kid could. "You said I could park Mrs. Warrington's Caddy. Please don't change your mind. I already got it halfway out the door and I didn't hit nothin' yet."

"You didn't hit anything yet." This probably wasn't the best time to correct Sydney's grammar, but the action was automatic. Besides, he couldn't have his daughter speaking like a heathen, now, could he?

Sydney must have realized they weren't alone because she grew quiet and came to stand beside him.

"Hi," she said to Amber, offering a friendly

smile. "My name's Sydney. Sydney Weston. How are ya today?"

The daddy in Jon couldn't help but feel a prideful tug inside. Sydney had never had a problem with shyness, that was for sure, and he'd taught her that amiability was a great way to secure the return business of customers.

Amber didn't respond, but that didn't stop Sydney. "You having car trouble?" the child tried again. "You've come to the right place, 'cause my dad can fix anything that runs on gasoline."

He indulged himself in just looking at his marvelous little girl who never ceased to cause a fuzzy, satisfied warmth to flow through him that only a "hand's on" kind of dad could feel. But his smile faded as he glanced back at Amber.

His mouth firmed into a fine line as he noticed her expression was nothing short of...earth-shattering.

Well what in heaven's name had Amber expected? A baby? Coming into town ten years after the child's birth, of course their daughter was going to be all grown up. A young lady, as his mother had described Sydney earlier. Had Amber anticipated meeting a toddler or something? Why did she look so astounded?

Amber's brown eyes seemed to roil with storm clouds as she studied Sydney. When she lifted her gaze to his, it was filled with silent, thunderous questions he found quite bewildering. Then her attention clamped once again on their daughter.

Finally she uttered a soft, breathy, "Oh, my," turned on her heel and raced toward her car. In another moment, she gunned the engine and was speeding away.

"Wow," Sydney said when the wheel-flung pebbles in the parking lot settled. "What was *her* problem?"

Jon didn't answer. Not because he meant to ignore his daughter's query, but because he didn't quite know what to say.

It wasn't his fault that Amber Holloway was having trouble facing her daughter. It wasn't his fault she couldn't cope with what she'd done in the past. And it wasn't his fault she felt the need to once again flee from her responsibility.

However, his silence was more telling than he'd realized.

"You know her, don't you, Dad?"

All he could do was look down into Sydney's chocolate-brown gaze.

"So, who is she?" Sydney asked, already sensing the answer to her first question.

Heaving a weary sigh, Jon debated what to say. How to answer. He could lie. Tell the child he had no idea who the crazy woman was. But Amber Holloway would probably be back. Of course, it was entirely possible that she'd run away again, just as she'd done before, and he and Sydney would never see hide nor hair of her. But she certainly wouldn't leave town before causing him as much trouble as she could. That was about how his luck ran. However, he refused to allow Amber to damage the trust he knew his daughter placed in him, so telling the child the truth and helping her deal with it was probably the best path to follow.

"That," he said with a slow, measured reluctance, "was your mother."

* * *

The faint odor of cigarette smoke hanging in the still air was plain evidence that the hotel clerk had made a mistake in booking Amber's room. She'd specified a smoke-free room. But the idea seemed so small it was practically meaningless when weighed against the gargantuan revelation that had thrown her into complete and utter turmoil.

She paced the seven steps it took to reach the far wall, then turned and paced back to the door of the tiny bathroom.

Her baby daughter hadn't died.

Her baby daughter hadn't died.

Raking all ten fingers through her hair, Amber paused in front of the dressing mirror and stared at her reflection as she was lambasted with questions and ideas that seemed to fly at her like dive-bombing fighter planes.

How could this have happened? How could a woman give birth and...

She stopped the thought in midstream. She hadn't been a woman. She'd been a girl. A teenager. Still how could *any* female, of *any* age, give birth to a baby and not know that her daughter lived? Such a thing was inconceivable... wasn't it? Things like that didn't really happen. Those kinds of situations were only impossible, unbelievable fictionalized ideas thought up by movie-of-the-week scriptwriters.

Things like this simply didn't happen to sane, rational, *normal* people like her.

At the moment, though, Amber felt anything *but* sane and rational.

Sydney.

Sydney Weston.

Staring unblinkingly into the mirror, Amber saw an older version of the child's face. Sydney had her eyes. Sydney had *her* nose. *Her* mouth. *Her* chin. *Her* hair.

There was no doubt in her mind that Sydney was her baby.

Her daughter was alive!

And Amber had run from her the instant she'd made the connection. Her eyes rolled upward and she closed her lids. Why had she made such a dash for her car? Why hadn't she simply stayed and talked things out with Jon? Why hadn't she introduced herself to her daughter?

She had no other excuse except to say that the discovery had been staggering. No, it had been mind-blowing. A literal bombshell that had demolished her thinking processes.

Alive. And well. And living with her father in Pine Meadow.

How could this be? How could this have happened?

Worrying the small pearl pendant that hung on

the delicate gold chain around her neck, Amber resumed her pacing.

Had Jon somehow kidnapped Sydney from the hospital in Connecticut where Amber had given birth?

She knew that Jon had been rebellious in his youth, but she'd never witnessed him break the law. Besides, the idea that he might have abducted their child simply didn't make sense when she thought of the awful accusations he'd made when she'd come to him with the news of her pregnancy.

"You won't trap me into marriage," he'd railed at her.

His choice of hurtful words had clearly told her that he didn't want her. That he didn't want their baby. So she really couldn't imagine him turning around and stealing their child from the hospital nursery.

Furthermore, even if Jon had been the type of person who could do such a thing, with doctors and nurses milling around, she just didn't think it would be easy to pull off. No matter what the movie-of-the-week scriptwriters might want TV watchers to believe.

But the Westons were wealthy enough to pay off a

doctor or nurse. The thought floated eerily into her mind, and she shivered.

People who chose to work in the medical profession did so to help people, not hurt them, she reminded herself. *Yes, but*, a tiny voice piped in, *there was always someone who was desperate enough to act unethically. Especially if enough money was involved.*

Suddenly Amber felt sick to her stomach to think the man she'd thought had been the love of her life would hurt her so terribly. Would rob her of her own flesh and blood.

He had been vicious when he broke up with you all those years ago, the voice echoed in her head.

Yes, she remembered. He had been cruel.

She unwittingly nibbled the cuticle of one thumb. Why didn't things seem to add up? she wondered. Why didn't the pieces fit?

The scene at Jon's garage earlier today unfolded again in her mind. All afternoon she'd been replaying the bit where Sydney had come into the picture. Her gorgeous little girl had stepped out of the driver's seat as if she'd been born there, Amber couldn't help but smile.

However, she forced herself to push the endearing image aside and focus on what had happened prior to Sydney's appearance. What had she said to Jon? More importantly, what had he said to her?

"So," his words floated into her mind, *"you've finally come to see how your little puppy dog has fared after all these years."* Her breath caught as his meaning cut her to the quick. Then, she remembered him saying, *"I'm not talking about me. I'm talking about the little stray you so heartlessly sent back to me. The runt you thought was so useless you didn't even give her a name before you got rid of her. "*

The realization was enough to make her knees buckle, and she sank onto the mattress, burying her face in her hands.

Jon thought she hadn't wanted Sydney. He'd thought she'd heartlessly sent her newborn daughter away without even giving the child a name. He thought she hadn't wanted to raise her own baby. He thought she'd known all along of her child's whereabouts, but that she hadn't even cared enough to call or visit or—

Amber groaned audibly. Dear Lord in heaven, Jon had thought all these horrible things about her for the last ten years! She pressed trembling fingers against her mouth as one final, chilling question came to her.

What must her little girl think of her?

Without another thought, Amber grabbed her purse and headed for the door.

* * *

"The garage is closed."

Amber spun around to see the same elderly lady with whom she'd talked before, the same one who had urged her, only a couple of hours ago, to stop in and visit Jon.

"Yes, I see that," Amber said, still wrestling with the disappointment she experienced over seeing the Closed sign hanging in the window of Jon's place of business. She'd had the thought of going to Weston House to look for him, but didn't know if she had the nerve to do that. "The sign there says he opens at eight in the morning."

She hated the thought of waiting all those hours before having the chance to talk to Jon. And Sydney.

A thrill shot through her body with a jolt when she realized all over again that her baby was alive. Really alive!

"Eight, sharp," the woman said.

Defeat rounded Amber's shoulders. "I guess I'll

come back tomorrow. Thanks for coming over to talk."

"Aww, now—" the woman actually seemed embarrassed "—there's no cause to go thanking me. Just trying to be neighborly. And seeing as how you sped out of here earlier like an arrow out of a bow, didn't seem like you and Jon had much chance to catch up on things."

"No." Now it was Amber's turn to feel chagrined. "You're right, we didn't." But she simply couldn't bring herself to explain the situation.

What could she say? That she'd just discovered today that she has a daughter?

This woman would think she was a raving lunatic! "Well, I'd better go find someplace to grab some dinner." The last thing Amber wanted was food. But she needed a means to politely take her leave. She had a hotel room floor that needed pacing, hours that needed worrying through. She turned away and started toward her car.

"You know..."

Something in the woman's tone made her jerk to a halt and spin around. The elderly lady's mouth was curled into a soft smile.

"I know how you can contact Jon," she said. "If you've a mind to, that is."

Amber's silent, eager expression was answer enough to make the woman chuckle.

"You see, Jon has his cell phone number listed there—" she pointed to a discreet, index-card-size note taped in a lower corner of the window "—just in case of an emergency. I had to call him once when a bunch of boys were hanging about in the parking lot here and getting up to no good."

With her hopes soaring, Amber rushed to the window, scrambling in her purse for her phone.

"Thank you," she told the woman, creating a new contact. "Thank you so much."

She shrugged. "I didn't do you any favors. His number is there in the window for all the world to see."

Amber protested, "Yes, but—"

"Would you stop already," the woman said, swiping the air with both hands. "I'm going to leave you alone so you can make your call."

"Thanks." Amber hit the call button, unable to wait until the woman was out of earshot.

Jon answered on the third ring, the sound of his voice like a soft caress against her ear.

"Jon," she said, making every effort to speak smoothly, "it's Amber."

There were several seconds of dead silence.

Finally she heard him exhale in a short, puffy sort of sigh.

"I've got to admit," he said quietly, "you've surprised me again. I thought I might hear from you, but not quite so soon. How'd you get my number?"

Not wanting to get the elderly lady who had helped her into hot water, Amber only told him half the truth. "I'm at your garage. You've got your contact number on an emergency card posted in the front window."

"Ah."

The small sound was velvet soft over the phone.

"And you thought this constituted an emergency."

Amber listened hard, but detected no censure in his tone, and she decided this was his way of filling what would have otherwise been an awkward silence.

"It is to me," she told him. "We need to talk, Jon."

Again, he sighed, but this one was tinged with irritation.

"Look," he said, "this isn't a good time. I'm trying to get dinner. And thanks to my mother, Sydney has a boatload of make-up work that needs to be done before school tomorrow. It isn't a good time for you to be coming over here and disrupting Sydney's life—"

"I have no intention of disrupting anything," Amber said, cutting in. "I swear to you, I don't." It broke her heart to hear him talk of cooking dinner and helping with homework so mundanely when she'd never had the opportunity to do such things for her daughter.

"Jon..." The pleading in her voice was so thick, she had to stop.

All she wanted to do was make him understand. But if she were to simply blurt out the situation; that she'd been lied to, that she'd thought all these years that their baby was dead, that someone had committed a horrendous crime by stealing her child, he'd think she'd gone completely insane. She needed to see him face-to-face. She needed to tell him everything in a calm, rational manner. That was the only way to make him understand she was telling the truth.

Before she could speak, he said, "I want you to

know that I won't allow you to upset Sydney. I don't want you overwhelming her."

"I understand," she said. "I don't want to overwhelm her, either."

She'd never dream of causing her daughter one moment of worry or trouble.

"M-maybe," she stumbled over her thoughts as they came at her, "it would be best if you and I met. Just to talk. To catch up."

Weariness pervaded the third sigh he expelled.

"I told you, Amber. I'm in the middle of fixing dinner. And then there's Sydney's schoolwork. I want to be here if she needs me."

"Of course," she quickly agreed. "But maybe after? There's a coffee shop down the street from your garage. In the same building where my dad had his shop. We can talk there."

"It'll be at least two hours. And I don't know if I can find a sitter."

"I'll wait," she said in a rush.

She heard yet another exhalation.

"*Please*, Jon. Please try." She could think of nothing else to say except, "I'll be waiting," and then she disconnected the call before he could reject her plea.

Chapter Three

He wasn't coming.

Absently Amber tapped the teaspoon against the palm of her hand. She glanced at the door of the small coffee shop for what surely must have been the millionth time.

Her eyes latched onto the large-faced clock behind the wide, white counter. Ten after nine. Nearly three hours had gone by since she'd called Jon. Without thought, she raised her thumb to her mouth and searched nervously for a cuticle to worry.

He wasn't coming.

But he wouldn't *not* come. Would he? Not after the way she'd pleaded with him. Not when she'd just discovered—

"Here you go," the waitress said softly, setting a

tall, icy glass of lemonade in front of Amber. "This is on the house. You won't sleep a wink tonight with all the coffee you've had."

A shadowy smile of appreciation barely curled the corners of Amber's mouth. Sliding the empty coffee mug away from her several inches, she murmured, "Thank you," and reached for the glass.

"I wish you'd let me bring you something to eat," the waitress said.

The concern she heard in the woman's tone surprised Amber. She was a complete stranger to the waitress. Only in a town as small as Pine Meadow would total strangers take such an interest in another's welfare, she thought.

"Thanks," Amber said, noticing that the woman's name tag identified her as Sue. "But I couldn't eat a thing."

Sue's distress deepened into creases that marred her brow. "Are you sure you gave him the correct address? I mean, is there any chance he might have gone to some other coffee shop? There's a diner on High Street... Maybe you should send him a text."

This time Amber's surprise had her mouth inching open, her eyes blinking. She'd guessed

Amber was waiting for someone. Waiting for a man.

Shifting her weight onto one hip, Sue absently slipped her pencil behind her ear, shook her head and said softly, "Honey, you're watching that door like you expect it to slip off its hinges and walk away. And no woman sits around for hours unless she's expecting a man. An *important* man."

The feathery-yet-intense inflection the waitress placed on the last short sentence clearly conveyed that she was sure that the man Amber awaited was no less than a lover. In any other circumstance, Amber was certain she'd have blushed. But the chaos reigning in her brain had her thoughts, her emotional responses, fragmented, splintered.

Jon *was* an important man, she realized. Not because of any close relationship she shared with him, but because of *what* they had created. A precious child. A daughter. Sydney.

The beautiful name whispered across her mind, and Amber latched onto it, focused on it and enjoyed a small moment of calm.

But the mere idea that her daughter was alive and well soon had her head churning all over again. However, she knew getting lost in the questions wouldn't help her one bit, so shoving the nerve-wracking thoughts aside, she looked up at the waitress.

"He *is* important," Amber admitted, although she didn't feel up to straightening out the woman's erroneous thinking by clarifying all that her statement suggested.

"Well, you wait as long as you like," Sue told her. "We don't close 'til eleven."

The front door opened then, and Amber and the waitress were turning their heads to look before the small bells attached to the door's hinge barely had time to tinkle.

He looked good, Amber mused, her pulse pumping to life through veins that suddenly felt too small. Even though trouble clouded his eyes, the intense green of them had her breath catching in her throat. She remembered years ago how the long, wavy hair at the back of his neck would curl in silky tresses around her finger. But his chestnut hair was cut shorter now. In a more respectable fashion.

"Jon! What brings you out at this time of night?" Sue greeted. "You're usually home with Sydney, doing homework and housework, playing Daddy."

Amber didn't know why she was so taken aback that the waitress knew Jon—his shop was just up the block from the coffeehouse—but startled she was. However, maybe it wasn't so much that the waitress knew him, but the familiarity with which the woman greeted him that had Amber feeling so... odd.

Jealousy.

When she put a name to the emotion that was constricting her chest, she nearly gasped. Impossible! It was completely out of the question.

Then what was it?

Despite the anxiety shadowing his gaze, Jon smiled at the waitress—and it was then that Amber correctly identified what she was feeling.

Envy. She was pea green with it. Before she could analyze the feeling further, though, Jon's intense gaze was once again focused on her, silently demanding her attention.

"Let's go," he said, keeping the door propped open with one hand.

Amber felt as if she moved in slow motion as she made to rise. A small exhalation of shock erupted from the waitress. Looking up at the woman, Amber saw questions in Sue's eyes.

You've been waiting for Jon? her gaze seemed to ask.

As if she were in a sleep-fogged dream, Amber

decided she simply couldn't concern herself with the woman's curiosity. Tossing some bills on the table, she turned toward the door.

"I've got a fresh apple pie in the back," the waitress said to Jon. "You sure I can't talk you into having a slice?"

"Some other time, Sue," Jon said. "Sydney's with a sitter, and she won't go to bed until I get home and put my foot down. But thanks anyway." Then his gaze darted to Amber and he curtly repeated, "Let's go," his tone urging her to hurry.

The waitress softly called, "Bye."

And Amber was surprised to realize she was the one being spoken to. She nodded to the woman and offered her a distracted smile as she moved toward Jon.

He was holding the door open and she was forced to brush the broad expanse of his chest with her shoulder as she passed between him and the doorjamb. The woodsy aroma of his cologne struck her full force and her instinct urged her to hesitate, to savor his heated scent. But luckily, he planted his hand firmly on the small of her back and propelled her out onto the sidewalk. Normally she'd have been incensed by such overbearing behavior, but she was relieved to follow his lead at the moment. How idiotic would she have looked if she'd paused to sniff the air as she'd passed him?

The sight of him after so many years, the smell of him, the feel of his strong hand planted low on the small of her back, was all enough to send her senses into a tailspin.

Get a grip, girl!

"I don't need the whole town knowing my business," Jon said, evidently in an effort to explain their rushed exit from the coffee shop.

"I understand," she automatically murmured, although she didn't really. Everyone in Pine Meadow already knew he had a daughter. People must realize the child had a mother. But she wasn't up to arguing. Not at the moment, anyway.

The whole world felt unbalanced. Off-kilter. But then, maybe it was just her. Of course, it was. Taking a deep inhalation of the cool night air, she tried to ground her thoughts, tried to stabilize her emotional equilibrium. But success was out of reach, she feared, because too much was happening too fast. She'd waited for him for hours. Hoped and prayed he'd come. Now that he had, she couldn't get a grasp on the situation. It was so unlike the normally cool, collected Dr. Amber Holloway.

"Like I told Sue," Jon said, "Sydney won't go to bed until I get home. I could text her threats until my thumbs bleed, but it won't do any good." He gave his wristwatch a darting glance in the dim light of the street lamp. "I can give you twenty minutes. Thirty, tops."

"I understand," she repeated.

"We can walk, or we can drive."

Again she parroted, "I understand."

His steps slowed. "Well—" then he stopped, lifting one hand palm up "—which will it be?"

The irritation she heard in his voice made her look into his face. There were lines bracketing his frowning mouth, and Amber had to fight the impulse to reach up and trace them with her fingertip. He looked so good. So ruggedly handsome. And that gorgeous green gaze, so full of—

"Amber!"

She jerked to attention. "I'm sorry, Jon." Reaching up, she swiped her hand across her face. She tipped up her chin, looked him in the eyes, and she repeated the apology a second time.

"You're acting like you're in a daze," he said. "What the hell is your problem?"

Anger reared its ugly head like a coiled and cornered snake, and it made her strike, viper-swift.

"How can you ask me that?" she said furiously, the dreamlike fog clouding her brain dissolving in the heat of her ire. "Do you have any idea what I'm going through here? Any idea what I'm dealing with?"

"Actually, I don't," he said.

There was no trace of annoyance or anger in his quiet voice. If anything, he simply sounded weary.

"I have no idea what's happening with you," he continued. "No idea what brought you back to Pine Meadow. But I'm sure I'm about to find out."

What brought her back to Pine Meadow? She stopped on the sidewalk and turned to face him.

Her father's death—and the discovery of the mysterious bank account—was what had her returning to her hometown. Fuzzy thoughts hovered at the edge of her brain... snatches of ideas that needed connecting, but they flitted just out of reach. She dismissed them, intent on focusing on the situation at hand.

But it wasn't her father's death she'd been referring to when she'd asked Jon if he understood what she was dealing with. She'd meant that she was facing the awesome realization that she had a child. A daughter. Sydney.

Was Jon purposefully missing the point just to shake her, make it utterly impossible to deal with him, with the situation she found herself in?

But, no, she thought, nearly shaking her head, he wasn't intentionally misconceiving anything. She remembered that he was under the impression that she'd abandoned Sydney ten years ago. He didn't know that she had had no idea that her daughter was alive and living with her father in Pine Meadow.

"So what's it going to be?" he asked. "A walk? Or a drive?" He made no effort to hide his frustration.

Her heart rate accelerated. So did the thoughts, questions, and doubts that bombarded her mind. Only moments ago in the coffee shop, Amber had felt a distinct delay of time, as though she were sleepwalking through a dream. But now the cadence of her existence seemed to speed up, his questions threatening to suck her into some churning chaos. Why would a simple decision throw her into such a panic? A walk or a drive. The choice wasn't life-altering.

"My car is right here." She pointed at the curb.

"Fine," he said. "A drive it is."

He approached the passenger door, opened it, and when she didn't move, he glanced at her. He tapped his wristwatch. "Thirty minutes, Amber," he reminded her.

His words, his body stance, his facial expression, even his deep green eyes, were all coated with a heavy layer of irritation that pulsed from him in palpable waves. The swells rippled, crested and crashed into her, driving her into motion.

"I understand," she said, digging into her purse for her car fob as she rounded the rear of the car.

Thirty minutes! How could she ever ask him all the questions strafing her mind like a spray of bullets from an unrelenting machine gun? Should she focus only on Sydney? Taking advantage of every second of the half hour allotted her to catch up on the last ten years of her daughter's life? Or should she start off by trying to convince Jon that she hadn't known of Sydney's existence?

"The car can't move until you start the engine," he told her.

The impatient edge that clipped his words only caused her nerves to become even more frayed. "Of course," she said.

She pressed the ignition button and cranked the engine to life. After slipping the car into gear, she glanced over her shoulder and pulled onto the street— and immediately realized that choosing to take a drive had been a terrible mistake. How could she possibly operate the car, deal with the stimulus of the passing scenery, watch for pedestrians, traffic signs and stoplights *and* take part in a complicated, in-depth conversation with Jon? The notion was ridiculous at best, dangerous at worst.

Luckily she was traveling in the direction of Jon's shop and she released an audible sigh of relief when the building came into view.

"Would you mind," she said, braking at the stop sign, "if I parked?"

He followed her gaze and evidently understood her intent.

"Whatever," he said.

She pulled into the lot and shifted the gear stick into Park, but before she cut the engine, she glanced over at him.

The dashboard lights threw green light over his face and hair, his chest, shoulders and arms. His eyes were trained, unwavering, on his shop, his chin lifted, his jaw square and stubborn. Silence surrounded him like a thick stone wall. He wasn't going to make this easy, that was clear to her.

And then she detected the heady scent of his

cologne floating on the still air inside the car. Her blood pulsed faster. The temperature seemed to rise in the close space, and she felt the impulse to lift the heavy weight of her hair up off the back of her neck to cool her skin, but she remained motionless.

Helplessly her gaze raked across his powerful chest, and an unbidden image flashed before her eyes: her young and trembling fingers splayed against his naked pectorals, her heart pounding fearfully, excitement thrumming through her body, the first time he'd tugged her on top of him during a passionate lovemaking episode.

She shook her head, banishing the erotic memory from her mind.

So, she thought, her mind whirling, where was she to start? She felt the seconds ticking by like a bomb about to explode—a bomb that might not harm her, but would surely whisk Jon away and with him all the important information about Sydney for which she was so desperate.

"Tell me about her."

Her whispered request sounded loud in the tight, suddenly airless confines of the car.

He said nothing, and for a moment Amber

feared he meant to refuse her request. But then he spoke, his gaze forward, his spine stiff.

"She's a great kid. She's healthy. Happy. She's... a great kid."

Amber sat, breathless with anticipation as she waited for him to continue.

But he didn't.

After a long moment, she said, "Is that all you're going to say?"

Did she detect a tremor in his long, controlled sigh? But she didn't have time to reflect on the thought before he turned his head to gaze at her.

"What do you want from me, Amber?" he asked. "What is it you're looking for?"

"W-why," she stuttered, dumbfounded that he could even ask those questions, "I want to know... *everything*. I want to know what she looked like when she was a baby. I want to know when she took her first step. Smiled her first smile. What word she first spoke. I want to know when she lost her first tooth. When she stopped believing in Santa Claus. What her favorite—"

"Ahhh, I see now," he cut in, his tone filled to the brim with ugly sarcasm. "You want to be filled in on all those years you missed."

"That's exactly what I want."

Hostility strained and condensed the already cramped space in which they found themselves. His green eyes narrowed as he glared at her. Amber couldn't actually see it, she *felt* it.

"You don't deserve to be given any information," he said, his tone tight, barely controlled. "You *chose* to separate yourself from Sydney. You *chose* to send her back to Pine Meadow. You *chose* to have nothing whatsoever to do with—"

"I chose none of those things!" she cried. She bit her bottom lip. This wasn't how she'd wanted to tell him. This wasn't how she'd meant for him to learn of her innocence. Smoothing her tongue across her lips, she inhaled, steeling herself to explain.

"I didn't know, Jon," she told him. "I didn't know my daughter was alive. Not until today. Not until—"

"You honestly don't expect me to believe that, do you?"

Even though she'd just moistened her lips, they felt as dry as road dust. "I expect you to believe it," she said, "because it's true."

"Yeah, right," he murmured, turning his head to glance out the window. After a quick moment, he swiveled back to look at her through the gloom.

His exhalation was short, audible, and full of disgust.

"When I think about what you did, how you sent Sydney packing, it makes me sick to my stomach. It infuriates me."

His words were like razor-edged knives hacking at her heart. But she refused to allow him to wound her with his opinion of her. Not again. He'd done it before. Ten years ago when she was just a tender, innocent teen. She refused to let him hurt her again with his asinine assumptions.

"If you insist on believing that I would do such a thing—" She halted, the unspeakable words lumping in her throat. A small cough cleared a pathway so she could proceed. "That I could knowingly, and willingly, give up a precious child, then by all means, go on believing it. It's no skin off my nose."

"None of this has been any skin off your nose, has it?"

She hated the fact that his sarcasm stung her so. "How can you say that? Think of everything I've missed!"

"All I can think of—"

His quiet tone was irritatingly unflappable.

"—is all that you've *gained*."

"All I've..." The two small words were all she was able to utter before her bewilderment over the hidden meaning of his statement had her frowning in silence. What on earth could he possibly mean?

The night seemed to grow bleaker, more shadowed. But she was still able to see him reach out in the darkness. His touch could almost have been described as a caress as his fingertips trailed a slow moving path along the dashboard's rounded edge. She remembered vividly what it was like being on the receiving end of his gentle touch. Her heart tripped in her chest, heat flickering to life deep in the very center of her being.

Stop!

"Nice wheels," he commented. "Still has that new car smell."

Amber tensed. What was he getting at? she wondered warily.

"Smells of something else, too," he continued. "Money."

Something inside her shriveled at the acerbity evinced in his tone. Why shouldn't she have a nice car? She'd worked long and hard. For years. Gone without for the sole purpose of her education. The automobile hadn't been that pricey. And it wasn't as if she'd paid cash. She was making payments.

Just like almost everyone else who bought a new car. Credit, the good ol' American standby. Another point in her favor, she thought, was that she hadn't made the purchase until she'd procured the job with the family medical practice.

"Too much money," he went on, "for the salary of say, a waitress like Sue, or a grocery clerk, or a shoe salesperson."

Blinking in the darkness, Amber knew he was just gearing up for an attack, but she still didn't quite see where he was heading with his argument.

Then he turned to face her. "Professionally manicured nails. That silk getup. Leather pumps." He added as an aside, "Italian imports, from the look of them." Hesitating only a moment, he asked, "Tell me, Amber, what do you do for a living?"

Even though she hadn't a clue why she should feel ashamed, her face flamed at the mysterious connotation concealed in what he said. She did her own nails, thank you very much! And she'd never in a million years admit to him that *he* had been her reasoning behind splurging on the new dress and shoes. The mere idea that she might meet Jon in Pine Meadow had her spending two careful hours selecting this dress, these shoes. But now she fervently wished she'd worn nothing more than her faded jeans, an old sweater and her comfortable, ratty sneakers.

He didn't give her time to answer his questions before he suggested, "Corporate executive? Stock investor? Lawyer?" His tone deepened as he said, "Whatever you do, it takes an education. And knowing your father and his inflexible plans for you, you've done nothing but focus on yourself. Your education and your career. So what you've gained, I'd say, is ten years free from the hassles and responsibilities of child rearing so you could set yourself up."

She actually gasped softly when he'd finally revealed his bitter gripe against her. Even though she'd promised herself she wouldn't allow him to hurt her, hot tears stung her eyes. She'd be damned if she let him see her cry.

"Set myself up? You're crazy." She was pleased that the pain and insult caused by his accusations wasn't evident in her voice.

"So answer my question," he quietly taunted. "What do you do for a living that allows you to afford this beautiful car and the expensive clothes?"

Earning her medical degree had made her feel more proud than any other accomplishment. But now Jon succeeded in making her feel lousy about it. He made it seem as though she'd tossed aside her child to get where she was. That simply wasn't true. But Jon wasn't going to believe that.

Finally she forced herself to admit, "I'm a doctor. A medical doctor."

"Ah…"

Amber detested the haughtiness he expressed, "…four years of college, four years of med school," he said. "Couple years of residency and you're set for life. That's about how it works, isn't it?"

Amber was confident she could hide her hurt feelings, but letting his blatant censure go without an argument was beyond her.

"I would never, ever have put myself before my daughter," she said, her throat feeling raw and painful. "If I had known—"

"Come off it, Amber," he cut in. "How could you not know? That's just plain crazy. Don't sit there and lie."

"I'm not lying," she insisted. "And I intend to prove it."

"How can a woman give birth and not realize whether or not her child lived?"

The blood in her veins seemed to slow as guilt froze it into icy slush. She whispered, "Don't you think I've been asking myself that same question all afternoon? All evening? Ever since I saw that little girl's face, I've been..." She swallowed hard, let the rest of the sentence fade as she bit down on her bottom lip and turned to look out into the night. In an instant she was thrown back into the past.

Heavy sheets of rain had been falling the night she'd gone into labor. Fear was what she remembered most. Fear. And soul-splitting pain. Oh, her father had tried to comfort her. The nurse and doctor, too. But the pain had been so intense it seemed to be never ending. The hours had ticked by at an agonizingly slow rate. She'd crooned over and over for the baby to come. Her cherished baby.

Through the months of her pregnancy, she'd wished and prayed for a baby boy. A baby boy who looked just like Jon. She knew her father would have had a fit if he'd known how she dreamed of her son's dark brown hair, his sea-green eyes, and a face that would remind her every single day of the man she desperately loved.

Yes, Jon had wounded her terribly with his hateful words, with his vicious rejection, but that didn't stop her from loving him. From wanting him. Since he refused to be with her, she'd spend her life raising the child they had created together. The child conceived through their love.

Her labor pains worsened, and the doctor grew worried and edgy. His anxious expression, his nervous demeanor, had frightened her more than the pain ever had. At last the doctor decided to take the baby through cesarean section rather than allowing her to give birth naturally. The last thing Amber remembered was calling out for her father and then pleading with the doctor to tell her what was going on, what was wrong with her baby. But her frantic, near delirious, questions, had gone unanswered as a nurse plunged a needle into Amber's vein and she'd slipped into a deep, unnatural sleep.

When she'd awakened, her father had been right there by her side, holding her hand. Oh, how she'd cried when he'd told her that her baby had been stillborn. But her grief had been relatively silent; hot, scalding tears had burned their way down her face as her father had patted her hand and whispered his consolation.

"This is all for the best. It's all for the best."

She'd only seen the doctor one other time when he'd come to check her sutures and release her from the hospital. He hadn't been able to look her in the eye. Amber had always thought that was because he'd felt badly that her baby had died. But now she knew better. Now she knew he'd been too ashamed to lift his gaze to hers, too embarrassed by the fact that he'd somehow stolen her baby from her.

Anger smoldered inside her chest. Anger at the years of grief she'd needlessly suffered. At her father for not protecting her. At the doctor for sneaking and conspiring. At all the years she'd lost with her little girl. At Jon for not believing her when she told him the truth.

"You can't argue with the cold, hard facts," Jon said, drawing her from the past. "You left Pine Meadow and seven, and a half months later you sent Sydney back." He sighed. "I'm not saying it was all your fault. You were young. I'm sure your father talked you into—"

"Don't you speak ill of my father." The animosity she heard in her own words startled her.

"But he was so adamantly against—"

"He's dead, Jon," she told him bluntly. "My father is dead."

A moment of silence followed the bombshell she dropped.

Jon smoothed his fingers over his chin in evident

contemplation. Finally he said, "I'm sorry, Amber. I'm truly sorry for you." His tone softened. "Ever since you left the shop this afternoon, I've been racking my brain trying to figure out why you came back. *Why did she wait ten years?* I kept asking myself. Well—" he paused, looking at her across the darkness "—now I know."

There they were again, Amber noticed. Those fuzzy, disconnected thoughts fluttering, moth like, at the outer edges of her brain. Ideas that needed piecing together like a jigsaw puzzle. Notions that had to do with her father and the reason she'd returned to Pine Meadow.

"Your dad's death," he began slowly and then faltered. "His dying has made you want to make things right, is that it?"

It hadn't been her father's death that had brought her back to Pine Meadow. *It had been the bank account!* The huge amount of money sitting in Weston Banking and Trust.

All the pieces were there, floating before her closed eyelids. Her father. Her daughter. Her lover. A large sum of money. Ten missing years. Blood whooshed through her ears as her panicked heart accelerated to a frantic beat.

It had been quite natural to make the doctor

who had delivered her baby the conniving, evil culprit. She'd never have suspected her father would have been a party to anything so horrible, so sinister. Her father had loved her. Hadn't he?

The pieces of this awful puzzle hovered and spun, just waiting to be snapped together.

Her eyes went wide as she looked at Jon. Had he been part of the plot to steal away her child? she wondered. Had the whole world been against her all those years ago?

Feeling her hands begin to shake violently, she grasped the steering wheel to steady them, but not before Jon's frown alerted her that he'd noticed how she trembled.

He was waiting for her to answer his question, but for the life of her, she couldn't remember what that question was.

She needed time. She needed space. She needed to think. Clearly. She needed to figure out this mess. She desperately needed to get away from Jon. Now.

"You have to go," she blurted, barely holding herself together. "I need time to process all of this. My mind is spinning. Your car is just up the block. A two minute walk. You should go."

"But—"

"Sydney's waiting," she reminded him. Her composure was slipping, slipping. "Surely our thirty minutes are up. We'll talk some more. Tomorrow. I'll come to your shop. While Sydney's at school."

He'd evidently become so wrapped up in their conversation that he'd forgotten all about the time. Darting a glance at his watch, he said, "Well, I really should—"

"Go," she told him, her tone firmer, louder than she'd intended.

After a short, bewildered nod of farewell, Jon got out of the car and walked away. Amber watched him in the rearview mirror until his form became obscured by the darkness.

Finally she could hold on no further. "Oh, Daddy, how could you?" she whispered. Then she buried her face in her hands and wept.

Chapter Four

Her father had sold her baby.

Amber sat in the car for an eternity feeling stunned and empty. She sat there until the air grew stuffy and stale. She sat there until there were no more tears in her to shed.

How could something so horrific happen to her? she wondered.

Her father had sold her baby.

The idea had floated in and out of her brain dozens of times yet she still couldn't quite seem to grasp it. The concept was simply too huge, too awful. She couldn't get her hands, or her mind, around it.

Her father had loved her. Had sacrificed so much for her. Cared for her. Nurtured her. To think that he'd purposefully taken away what would have been the most precious thing in her life—*and he'd profited from the act*. It was simply unfathomable.

When she'd found the bank account and all those unopened statements, she hadn't known what to think.

The notion that her father had accepted money from Jon's parents for taking her out of town, out of their son's life, had been the most logical conclusion. But now... after seeing Sydney with her own eyes, realizing that her child hadn't been stillborn, but stolen...

No, she told herself firmly, finally finding the guts to admit the truth. Not stolen. *Sold.* By her father. Her own flesh and blood. There could be no other explanation for that large sum of money sitting in Weston Savings and Loan under an account listing her father as owner.

But who had supplied the money? Jon's parents? His tyrannical father, his overbearing mother? Or had Jon been the buying partner in the torrid baby-selling bargain?

He was Sydney's father. He had the most to gain by offering Amber's dad a deal. Maybe Jon had decided he hadn't wanted to live his life with the daughter of a shoe repairman, a girl from the wrong side of town, a girl with no gentility climbing around in her family tree, a girl with no prospects, no future. Maybe he had decided he hadn't wanted his child's mother, but he had wanted his child. That would make perfect sense.

But wait! her subconscious silently nudged her. Why would Jon make such an angry fuss, insisting that she knew all about Sydney? That she'd sent the child back to Pine Meadow without a second thought?

A smoke screen, pure and simple. He wanted to cover his horrible deed. And making her feel guilty, making her out to be the bad guy, was the perfect ruse.

But Jon Weston wasn't that kind of person. The statement whispered across her mind.

Amber heaved a sigh, reminding herself that ten years had passed. Anything could happen to a person over that amount of time. Besides, hadn't he changed even *before* she'd left Pine Meadow? Hadn't he rejected her with mean and hateful words that she wouldn't have believed could have come from him unless she'd actually heard them with her own ears?

She didn't know Jon. Didn't know who he was. Or who he'd become.

Tread carefully. The susurrus warning echoed in

her brain. *You don't know if he's guilty. You don't know for sure.*

No, she didn't, she admitted silently. But she meant to find out. And if she discovered he was behind this terrible, twisted mess, then she'd show him as much mercy as he'd shown her all those years ago.

None.

* * *

"Ya know, Dad," Sydney said, her voice small, "I'm feeling kinda queasy in my stomach."

Jon frowned and studied his daughter's face for signs of illness: flushed cheeks or a bleary-looking gaze. Maybe the headache Sydney suffered yesterday was a prerequisite of the flu or something. Funny how she hadn't mentioned feeling ill until now.

Their before-school ritual was already well underway. Sydney had eaten her breakfast, she'd picked out her clothes and changed into them, she'd made her bed. If she wasn't feeling well she usually announced that fact well before now, so Jon was surprised to hear her complain. But then, he thought, maybe he shouldn't have been. He had an idea what this queasy stomach was all about.

"You really should go to school today," he said, keeping any hint of censure out of his tone. His daughter had been hit with quite a surprise yesterday; what she needed was understanding, not an overbearing father breathing down her neck. "Thanks to your grandmother, you're all caught up, but if you miss another day of school..."

"Yeah—" Sydney rolled her eyes dramatically "—thanks to Grandmother I had two full pages of math problems to do and a chapter of social studies to review last night. I missed my favorite TV show and—"

"All right, now," he gently admonished. "Grandma only did what she thought was best for you."

The child giggled delightedly. "If she ever heard you call her *Grandma* she'd twist your ears into pretzels."

Jon grinned at his daughter's reflection in the mirror. "She probably would. So that's our little secret, agreed?" He reached out his index finger.

Automatically, Sydney curled hers around her father's and gave one quick, gentle tug. This had been their secret "handshake" for as long as Jon could remember. He picked up the hairbrush.

"So, what's it going to be today?" he asked, drawing the brush through her long red hair. "Leave it loose? Ponytail? Braids?"

"A braid, please," she told him. "Just one. Straight down the back."

"One braid, coming up." He parted Sydney's hair into three neat sections and began to plait. His fingers were deft and he executed the task with the ease of someone who had performed it time and again. He had. For as long as Sydney's hair had been long enough to braid. Oh, he hadn't always been as skilled as he was now. Sydney had worn more than one lopsided braid. But plaiting hair was like playing a musical instrument, cooking a perfect meatloaf, or tuning a car's engine—practice made perfect.

He enjoyed this early-morning ritual with Sydney. Fixing her breakfast and then cleaning up the dishes while she got herself dressed. He always brushed her hair, otherwise she would walk out the door with her bangs sticking straight up. He'd pack her lunch while she packed her book bag and then she'd kiss him goodbye before running for the big yellow school bus that stopped for her up the block.

Yes, he relished his mornings with Sydney, he thought, reaching for a fabric-covered elastic band he used to secure the tail end of the braid. These mornings helped him start his day with a smile. Even on days when he didn't feel like smiling. Days just like today.

He hadn't meant to hurt Amber's feelings last night when they had talked. All he'd been looking for was a little honesty. Did she really expect him to believe she had no idea Sydney was living in Pine Meadow? That was just ridiculous—

"Maybe," Sydney began haltingly, staring wide-eyed at him in the mirror, "I ought to go to the shop with you today."

Here it comes, Jon mused. That expression on her cute face, that breathy suggestion, both were packed to the hilt with turmoil. This had nothing to do with an upset stomach. This had to do with Amber. He'd have felt safe betting his last dollar on it.

"I think you need to go to school," he stressed, knowing full well an argument was brewing.

"B-but *what if she comes?*"

Awe, fear, and excitement churned in that small

whispered question. Jon realized it was only natural for Sydney to want to see her mother. He only wished he knew what was in Amber's head. What did the woman hope her visit to Pine Meadow would accomplish? He wouldn't allow Amber to hurt Sydney. That, he simply wouldn't tolerate.

"She probably will come to the shop today," he told Sydney.

The glow of expectation in her chocolate-brown gaze twisted his heart.

"But you, young lady," he said, "will be in school. Amber, er, ah," he stammered, then corrected, "your mother and I have some talking to do—"

"I want to see her."

Jon kept his voice calm, but insistent. "I know you do. And there will be plenty of time for that. *After* school."

"Ya mean it?" She actually squirmed with the anticipation. "Today?"

"Hold still," he said, hating the all-too-human feelings of possessiveness that reared up inside him. But he muscled them to the back of his brain, logically understanding that meeting Amber could very well be a wonderful event in his daughter's life. He brushed the tiny tail of the braid around his finger until it curled prettily and then patted her shoulder. "All done. Time to pack up your books. The bus will be by soon."

She hurried off toward the kitchen, as if rushing the day to begin would somehow make this afternoon arrive sooner. Anxiety knotted in his stomach as he weighed the possibilities of Sydney meeting her mother. Good experience, or bad, he knew everything hinged on Amber. He had no control over the woman and that worried him.

Jon was wrapping a cheese sandwich in plastic wrap when Sydney asked, "You don't think she'll leave town without talking to me at least once, do you?"

He didn't like the anxiety he saw marring her young brow. "Duh," he said, hoping his dopey tone would assuage her apprehension, "now why would she do a dumb thing like that?"

But Sydney's mouth remained a taut line as she shrugged. Then she said firmly, "You get her to stay at least until I get home from school."

A chuckle eased from his throat. "Honey, I don't expect I could get Amber Holloway to do anything that she didn't want to do."

He remembered a time that wasn't so. A time

when Amber would have done anything, gone anywhere, to please him. Hell, she'd have walked through fire if he'd given her the least indication that that's what would have made him happy. But that had been years ago. A whole other lifetime, really.

"But you're going to try, right?"

After a quick kiss on the cheek, Sydney went running out the door, and Jon was left alone in a houseful of troubled thoughts.

Amber Holloway. My, how that woman had changed his life. Well, she hadn't been quite a woman back then. Spindly teen would have been a more apt description, all elbows and knees, when he'd first met her. But then all those years ago he couldn't have been defined as anything other than lean and lanky, himself.

Reaching for his mug, Jon took a sip of steamy coffee, and smiled as he swallowed. He could picture the first time he'd seen her as if it were happening right this moment rather than years and years ago. He'd walked into her father's shoe repair shop looking for someone to put some new holes into his favorite black leather belt. His mother had given him such grief that morning, telling him to throw away the worn belt and buy a new one. But

Jon had been stubborn. He didn't want a new one. He saw his parents as extravagant and excessive when it came to buying new things, tossing their money around. So what if he'd lost a few pounds? Basketball season did that to a guy. All he needed were a couple of new holes in the belt and it would serve him just fine.

As he thought back on it now, Jon figured it was his desire to rebel against his mother and father about the stupid belt more than anything else that took him into Harry Holloway's shop. And the fact that the shop was located in the Bowers made it all the more perfect. Him patronizing a business located on the poor side of town would really tick off his parents but good.

The door of the shop stuck when he tried to open it, and he'd had to give it a good push. The air was dry and hot inside, the strong smell of leather and shoe polish hitting him like a solid wall. The girl behind the counter was young, the sun shining through the big front windows gleaming like molten fire against her long, wavy red hair. She smiled a hello, and unwittingly Jon's posture straightened, his shoulders squared.

Immediately, he'd been struck by his reaction. Why on earth would he feel the need to strut his stuff for this young colt-of-a-girl? She was too young for his interest. Much too young. Why, she couldn't be more than thirteen or fourteen. In the mind of a seventeen-year-old, a *high school senior* for goodness' sake, this girl was just a kid, and being attracted to a kid was worse than catching a case of Ebola virus.

But as he explained to her what he needed, and she took the belt from his hands, his gaze was drawn again and again to those twinkling, nut-brown eyes of hers, all that creamy skin speckled with tiny freckles across her nose and forehead. She was cute. There was no way around it.

They became friends from the very first. Secret friends. If Jon's buddies ever discovered that he spent many of his afternoons with a kid, they'd have ridiculed him into tomorrow. Many times he told himself he should stay away from her. But his motorcycle seemed to steer itself into the Bowers, seemed to park itself under the shady trees of the tiny little scrap of land the Pine Meadow planning board tried to pass off as a formal walking garden in the town's only park.

Amber Holloway was fourteen, she haughtily assured him. The proud manner in which her chin tipped up made him laugh, and she became angry.

But it didn't take much placating from him to make her smile again, though.

She was so easy to talk to, and she seemed to understand him. And his problems. Mainly his contempt for his parents. She didn't share it, didn't pass judgment. She simply understood. Jon could never have complained to his other friends. How could he? From their point of view, he was someone who was practically offered the world on a silver tray. Who was he to bemoan the expensive clothes he wore, the motorcycle he rode, the boarding school he attended? But Amber quietly listened and never criticized. She cared about him. At a time when he felt that no one else really and truly did. He liked that about her. He liked it a lot. And he guessed that was what kept him coming back to visit her in that pathetic little garden.

They were friends. Nothing more. And it was a relationship that they'd had to hide. From her father. From his parents. From his school buddies. But the times he spent with her were some of the most memorable of his life. He felt he could have told her anything. Everything. And he did.

For nearly eighteen months they met in secret. They talked and laughed and philosophized. They shared their experiences. They cried together.

They learned from each other, and grew. They knew everything there was to know about each other.

If he were to be completely honest, he'd have to admit that he had known Amber adored him. Almost from the very start. He saw it in the doe-eyed expressions she graced him with, in the way she hung on his every word. Yeah, he'd been aware that she loved him. That she wanted more from their relationship. From him. But he forced himself to keep their alliance a "friends only" kind of thing. Completely platonic. She was too important to him to mess up what they had with too much emotion. Besides, she was too young to take things to a higher level... a physical level. He promised himself he wouldn't allow it.

But each passing month made keeping his promise more and more difficult. He longed to caress her delicate, pale cheek, to kiss her soft, full lips. Still, he held tight to his silent pledge even though he knew Amber would have eagerly given herself to him.

Then on Amber's sixteenth birthday, Jon could stand it no longer and he offered to take her for a ride on his motorcycle. They had driven out to the dense woods on the outskirts of Pine Meadow.

That had been the day that had changed their relationship. Forever.

Jon sighed, and like the dust-kicking wheels of a hopped-up sports car, his memories spun away out of sight.

The teenage Amber had been gangly and thin, he remembered, she'd been awkward in her still-developing body, but she'd been the most caring and compassionate person he'd ever met. And she'd stolen his heart right from his chest.

He couldn't help but notice how the years had changed her. The woman who had stood in his parking lot yesterday afternoon, silky fabric softly draping luscious curves, short hemline revealing a mile of shapely legs, had been no less than utterly gorgeous. She was enough to cause a man to suffer restless insomnia, and he knew damned well she was behind all his tossing and turning last night. Even now, as he imagined her lush body, her softly curling red hair, her wine-colored lips, those deep mahogany eyes, that pert, little nose, he felt a wrenching, a tightening, down low in his gut.

Damn it! What the devil was the matter with him?

His chance with Amber was over. Long over. Any opportunity the two of them might have had together had been murdered—killed by mistakes both of them had made in the past.

Lust. That was it, he realized. Pure male lust.

So he had a yearning. So what? He could handle it. Certainly she wouldn't be in town for that long. A few days. A week at the most. He could control his physical desires.

He took a sip of his stone-cold coffee and grimaced. The clock on the wall made him curse under his breath, and he dropped the mug into the sink. Seven forty-five! And he wasn't even dressed yet. He rushed toward his bedroom, knowing full well that, for the first time since he'd opened the shop, he'd be unlocking the doors late. All because he'd sat dawdling over his memories of Amber Holloway.

* * *

"Well, ma'am," the young, suit-clad bank officer said. He'd introduced himself as Pete Taylor. "I really don't have any other information on the account. Other than what I've already given you, that is."

Amber sat back in the cushioned seat, depression quickly seeping into every pore. For some stupid reason she'd thought this morning's trip to Weston Savings and Loan would answer her questions. At least some of them. As it turned out, she was just as much in the dark about the money as she'd been when she'd walked through those thick, double-wide glass doors fifteen minutes ago.

"That's too bad," she told the man. "I'd hoped to find out where the money came from. You see, with my father's death last month—"

"I'd like to tell you again how sorry I am to hear that," Mr. Pete Taylor remarked automatically.

Amber murmured her appreciation. "I came upon the bankbook while going through his things. My father never said a word to me about this account."

The young man's brows raised in surprise. "It is odd that he didn't speak of this to you, especially since you're listed here as his beneficiary." He peered at the computer screen closer. "Another odd thing... the account shows no activity." He looked back at her. "I don't mean little activity. I mean none. Other than the accruing interest, there have been no deposits, no withdrawals." His mouth curled into a soft smile. "But this is really wonderful for you. A nice, tidy hidden treasure you've unearthed."

He might think so, but Amber certainly didn't. This money was more like a heavy boulder tied around her neck, a weight that seemed to grow heavier with each passing moment. For that reason, she didn't respond, but sat there, motionless.

Evidently becoming uncomfortable with the silence that had settled over them, the man cleared his throat, his smile fading, and he glanced back at his computer terminal.

"You know," he said, "this account is ten years old. I've only been with the bank for two years. I could call upstairs..."

Amber felt the hairs on the back of her neck prickle. *Upstairs* was sure to mean the executive offices of the bank.

"...I could talk to Mrs. Weston—she's the president of the bank—maybe she'll know something about your father's account."

"No." The word erupted from her lips so suddenly that the bank officer started. "No, thank you, Mr. Taylor," she said, this time with a little more decorum.

The very last thing in the world she needed right now was to have Helen Weston alerted to her presence in her bank. In her town. Oh, Amber hadn't fooled herself into thinking she could stay in Pine Meadow without the town's matriarch discovering her presence. She knew Jon's mother would find out, sooner or later. Amber just opted for later, was all.

Then she asked. "*Mrs.* Weston is the bank's president? When I lived in Pine Meadow, Mr. Weston was in charge."

Pete Taylor nodded. "He died a while back. It's been years now. Before I started working here."

"Oh." So Jon's father had passed away, too.

"Well..." Pete paused as if he was at a loss as to what to do next. Then his expression became once again animated as an idea evidently came to him.

"How about if I start the paperwork to have the account turned over to you?" he said. "You did bring a death certificate with you?" He looked at her expectantly.

"Yes, I did," she told him. "But..." Amber didn't understand why she hesitated, but something inside her vied for her attention, like two feet planted firmly on a car's brake pedal. "I'm not sure I want to do that just yet."

He seemed bewildered by her hesitance. His suggestion made sense, she realized. It was only logical for the account to be put into her name. But for some reason—

That money was tainted! The words came into her mind, loud and clear. That money was defiled. She didn't want to have anything to do with it.

She stood suddenly. "I'll be in town for a bit. I'll come back another day." Then she turned toward the door.

"Wait," he called.

The doorknob was still in her hand as she twisted to face him.

"At least take the paperwork with you." He reached into his drawer and pulled out a form. "Bring this in with the appropriate information filled in. And I'll need a copy of the death certificate." Then he further offered, "I have access to a copy machine, if that will help..."

He was so eager to please, she realized. She went to his desk, smiled and took the paper from him. "I do want to thank you. You've been most helpful."

"It's been my pleasure."

Back out in the bank's main lobby, Amber took a moment to exhale a disappointed sigh. This visit had been pretty close to useless.

The large, wide-open space of the bank lobby was built in an atrium fashion. One side of the room was lined with a high counter behind which smartly-dressed tellers made transactions for Pine Meadow residents and businesspeople. Several free-standing cubicles were arranged in the center of the room. An elegant staircase led to the second floor where office doors lined the wall directly above the teller counter. Amber couldn't seem to tear her eyes from the office doors lining the upper landing.

That, she knew, was the "upstairs" to which the bank officer had just referred. Those were the executive offices. A shiver coursed across her skin.

That woman.

Amber couldn't see Helen Weston sitting at a desk behind one of those heavy wooden doors, but that didn't matter. She could picture Jon's mother, just the same.

Thoughts of that woman conjured feelings in Amber that threatened to overwhelm her. The stern, disapproving Helen Weston had thought Amber worthless. *Less* than worthless. Amber, Helen Weston had thought, was a girl from the wrong side of town looking to get ahead by clinging to her son, and that was something that she simply wouldn't allow to happen. In the matriarch's eyes, the penniless daughter of a shoe repairman was not good enough for Jon. And because Helen Weston had thought it, voiced it, Amber had believed it. For a long, long time.

One of the office doors on the second floor opened, and a middle-aged woman stepped out onto the landing. Amber recognized Jon's older sister. The woman knocked on the door of the adjacent office. The door opened, and Helen Weston came into Amber's view.

Unwittingly she dipped her head, averting her face from view. She should leave the bank. Now. She should move one foot in front of the other, until she was standing out on the sidewalk. But paralysis seemed to have frozen her legs in place.

All she could think about was the huge sum of money that had been sitting in Helen Weston's bank for years. Amber thought of what that money had bought. What that money had cost her. Helplessly Amber glanced upward.

As though the elderly woman had some sixth sense and realized she was being watched, she paused in her conversation and glanced down at the lobby below. Her gaze scanned the sparse, quiet group of employees and patrons, and came to rest on Amber.

Immediately Amber cast her eyes to the floor, turning her face away.

Worthless. The word rang through her head. Less than worthless.

A blast of anger exploded inside her, rocking her from the top of her head to the very soles of her feet. How dare that woman make her feel inferior?

Yes, she might have been born and raised in near poverty. But that happened to lots of good-hearted, reputable people. And yes, she might be the daughter of a shoe repairman. But her father...

The thought faltered when her father—or rather, her father's behavior came to mind. Her father hadn't been honest. Hadn't been good-hearted. Hadn't been reputable. She'd just realized that last night. Amber felt her chin tremble.

Lord, she had to get out of this building!

But she stood firm as she felt something odd stir inside her. Whatever it was grew and stretched.

Determination. That's what it was.

She hadn't done anything wrong. She was a blameless victim in this mess. Besides that, she wasn't a mousy, easily frightened teenager any longer. She was a grown woman. An educated woman. A woman filled with a sturdy resolve to solve a horrible mystery—a mystery in which Jon's mother was most probably somehow embroiled.

Her shoulders squared, her spine straightened, and Amber lifted her chin slowly, raised her gaze until she was looking directly and steadily into Helen Weston's eyes.

I'm here! she wanted to shout. *I'm back in town. And I'm not leaving without telling my daughter the truth!*

But she wouldn't make a scene. It just wasn't in her. So, she simply stood there, letting the elderly woman get a good, long look at her. Only then did she walk out the door into the bright morning sunshine.

Chapter Five

Rounding the corner of the one-story brick building, she caught sight of him working under a shade tree and she stopped, deciding on a whim to give herself a moment to take stock of the situation; what she should say, how she should act.

She grimaced, her shoulders inching toward her ears. Who was she kidding? Amber mused, having enough sense to feel irritated by the blatant lie. Her objective in pausing wasn't to plan out a strategy—it was to stare at him, plain and simple.

He was poised over the open hood of a car, tinkering with the engine. The fabric of his cotton shirt was smooth across the broad expanse of his shoulders and his faded denim jeans defined hard thighs and a tight butt. She could no more stop the appreciative grin that tugged at the corners of her mouth than she could have stopped time itself.

You're not here for this, her logical mind chided from what seemed a far distance.

Oh, why don't you just shut up and enjoy the view? a fun-loving voice responded.

Clapping her fingers over her lips, she stifled the delighted chuckle that bubbled up into her throat. She hadn't heard a peep from the gleeful side of herself in... longer than she could remember. She'd been too focused on learning the anatomy of the human body and how it worked with the chemistry of modern medicine.

She'd only relished the sight of Jon's denim-clad rear for a few seconds when she watched his hand snake out toward the toolbox that was too far away from him. She knew that, any moment, he would have to lift up his head to locate the toolbox, and she was mortified to think she might get caught standing here gawking at him.

"Hello," she called, just as he straightened his back.

Fall had the air feeling clean and cool, but the leaves on the trees were still a vibrant green. Fingers of sunlight filtered through them now, burnishing Jon's brown hair with a rich chestnut hue. A strange thrill shot through her when he turned toward her, his striking emerald eyes settling on her face. However, just as she'd suppressed the laughter that had threatened to surface, she did the same to this giddy swell that rolled over her like an ocean wave. These emotions had no place here. No place at all.

"Amber."

Not even a hint of a smile softened the straight line of his mouth—the same mouth that, years ago, had been so gentle, so coaxing against hers, the same mouth that... Her hands balled into fists at her side. Her vivid sensuous memories of Jon were hampering her battle against the strong physical attraction she felt for him—the attraction she'd already decided she couldn't allow herself to feel.

When she realized that her name was all she was going to receive from him by way of a greeting, her shoulders sagged with a sigh.

"What can I say to convince you?" she asked quietly, struggling to focus on the problems of the here and now.

His brows arched. "Convince me?"

"Yes," she said. "What will make you believe I'm not a horrible person? That I'm innocent of wrongdoing?"

Jon was quiet for some moments. He centered his attention on the tools in the metal box. He reached in and picked up a ratchet of some kind and then set it back down in its allotted space. She remained silent, unmoving, determined to wait him out for an answer.

Finally he lifted his eyes to hers. "I don't know, Amber," he told her. "I'm not sure there's anything you can say that would convince me."

Her heart grew heavy, but she didn't speak.

"But I've been thinking about our conversation last night," he went on. "About our... disagreement. And I think it would be best if we just let it go for now. This shouldn't be about you and me. This shouldn't be about what did or didn't happen in the past. This is about Sydney. Period."

She studied his face. What he said made sense. Sounded mature. Wise. Now all she had to do was figure out if he was being honest and up-front with her, or if this was just more smoke he was blowing to cover up the truth about how their daughter came to be in Pine Meadow.

Whether this idea was more deception on Jon's part, or pure concern, it really didn't matter. Because what he said was the truth. Sydney was all that mattered to her. The rest could wait. She had plenty of time to discover the facts about the past.

"You're right," Amber said. "This is about Sydney. Period."

Her statement might have been described as a little misleading, but she didn't feel badly about that. She had a right to know the full, unadulterated circumstances surrounding the loss of her baby. And she had every intention of exerting that right. But she'd bide her time. For now, she was content to focus on Sydney.

"So," she began softly. "Did you tell her? About who I am, I mean?"

Jon's gaze didn't waver. "I told her."

"How did she react?"

Some fleeting, unreadable emotion passed over his face. Was that concern? A scowl of anger? A frown of worry? However, her building anxiety and excitement regarding her daughter didn't allow her to ponder Jon's emotional state for long.

"Well," she prompted him, suddenly feeling as eager as a newborn pup, "w-what did she have to say?"

His shoulder hitched up the merest fraction of an inch. "Sydney's an intelligent child. She's curious by nature."

The stoicism evinced in his tone didn't disguise his defensiveness. Her whole body relaxed, her heart softening, when she realized he felt threatened by her presence.

"I have no intention of coming between you and Sydney," she told him.

"That's good because that'll never happen."

There was a clear challenge in his voice, in the rigid set of his shoulders, his narrowed gaze. She couldn't help the contradiction he made in suggesting they avoid arguments by letting go of their differences, and now here he was egging for a fight.

As far as she could see, there were two avenues open to her; she could accept and become embroiled in the controversy he was offering, or continue to try to calm his fear—the fear that was the underlying cause of his harsh tone and the opposition in his green eyes. Because she could easily imagine what he must be feeling, and because she did like his idea of focusing on Sydney, Amber decided to continue along the pacifying route.

She offered him a small smile and softly said, "Then we agree." Her smile widened. "That's good, don't you think?"

It was immediately obvious that he sensed the olive branch she was extending. He averted his eyes, almost shamefully, and when he looked up at her again, he slowly nodded his agreement.

"Sydney can't wait to meet you," he admitted quietly. He shook his head, chuckling softly to himself. "So much so," he went on, "that she tried to get me to let her stay home from school today."

A rush of pure joy rolled over her. "She did?"

"Mm-hmm." He nodded again. "She complained of an upset stomach. But I knew she was just excited and nervous about meeting you. I told her she had to go to school, and that the two of you could talk this afternoon. After school was over."

Her daughter had wanted to skip school in order to meet her. The idea made her giddy with pleasure.

"I know what she means about having an upset stomach." Amber absently flattened her palm against her midriff. "I've had butterflies flapping inside me, too. But I am glad you made her go to school. I wouldn't like to be the cause of her missing a day." After a moment, she asked, "Does she like it? School, I mean?"

"As much as any kid, I guess," he said. "She hates

math, although she's pretty good at it. She likes history. Especially Egyptian history. Give her a book about Pharaohs and mummies and pyramids, and she'll read it, cover to cover." He reached for a tool from the toolbox and leaned over the engine. "'Course, she could be an honor student if she wanted to be..."

Amber moved closer, until she shared the shade of the tree with him.

"She's just decided she doesn't want to be."

An unwitting frown creased her brow as she placed her hands on the fender of the car and leaned forward an inch. What he said about their daughter bothered her.

Sydney was only ten. Much too young to realize the value of a good education. Amber remembered her own goals as a youngster; to postpone or skirt altogether any and all schoolwork she could. The only thing on a child's mind is playtime. Having fun with friends and gossiping on the telephone took precedence over everything and anything.

Her memory of Mrs. Jenkins was crystal clear. Her fifth-grade teacher had threatened to hold her back a year. She'd been mortified at the thought of being left behind by her friends. But worse, her father had been terribly upset. He'd grounded her for two full months until her next report card had proven that she'd gotten her grades back on track.

She blinked, studying Jon's profile. She didn't understand how he could be content to allow Sydney to choose her own achievement level. Was he doing all he could as a parent to see to it that Sydney got the best education possible? Amber's chest pinched painfully when she remembered all her own father had done, all he'd sacrificed, so that she could become a doctor.

However, following close on the heels of grief was an underlying bitterness that smothered everything else when she remembered that her father had sold her baby girl, had cost her all those years with Sydney. It was difficult for her to comprehend how she could still love her dad, still grieve for him, now that she knew what he'd done. She pushed the confusing thoughts aside.

"Sydney will turn things around," Jon commented. "She'll realize how important school is before too much longer. She'll come to understand what's best for her."

Maybe when she's thirty, Amber mused silently. Knowing what was truly best simply wasn't in a child's nature. Getting what was wanted was the number one priority.

But then, what made her an expert? What did she know about children? Only what she remembered from her own childhood. And who was she to come traipsing into Pine Meadow and start telling Jon how he should or shouldn't raise Sydney? However, if she didn't speak her mind, if she didn't tell Jon that she felt he ought to put a little pressure on their daughter regarding her schooling, what kind of mother did that make her?

Lord, this was so complicated. She decided it was best to leave it alone for now. To wait until she had more information before she butted heads with him over this. She'd be meeting Sydney this afternoon. Maybe then she'd have more facts on which to base her assumptions regarding Jon's skills as a father.

Hoping to steer the conversation to safer ground, she queried, "Does Sydney play a musical instrument? I played the flute when I was in grade school." A smile lingered on her lips. "I sang in the choir, too."

"She's not taking band," Jon said, pulling out a spark plug from its slot. "She's not taking chorus, either. Those are both extracurricular activities in her school, but she hasn't shown any interest."

Then he said, "Hand me the spark plug gauge out of the toolbox, would you?"

Automatically she picked up the circular metal disk with two manicured fingers. It was dull and dark with years of greasy use. She held it out to him.

"It's round," he told her, his attention still on the engine. "A little larger than a half dollar—"

He turned his face toward her then, saw that she'd already picked it up. A spontaneous chuckle of delight escaped from her when she saw the utter surprise registered in his eyes.

"I must have handed you this thing about a million times," she reminded him.

One corner of his mouth hitched up with the memory. "Yeah," he said softly, "I guess you did at that."

His smile was sexy enough to cause her blood to heat in her veins. He took the gauge from her, his fingers lightly brushing hers, and a strangely familiar hum vibrated across her skin, like a warm, exotic breeze on bare flesh. She successfully quelled the sharp inhalation of surprise and pure pleasure that welled up within her. Jon turned back to his work, and Amber was left wondering if he'd felt the sensual buzz that had shivered between them.

Jon glanced up at her, his eyes barely lighting on hers before he busied himself with the plug. But in that instant, she recognized awareness in his green gaze. He was conscious of the insistent pulse resonating between them. She was positive of it.

Her heart raced and perspiration prickled her brow even though the promise of autumn injected a crisp edge into the air. Her inward reactions to this... this magnetism were quite involuntary, and she was helpless against them. The increased heart rate, the elevated blood pressure, the feeling of pins and needles prickling every inch of her skin. She could do nothing to fight these physical responses to Jon. But that didn't mean she had to give in to them, or let him see what he was doing to her.

Knowing he, too, was aware of the intense humming, and that if he wasn't battling the same corporal reactions, he was at least feeling discomfited by the awkwardness, she decided to do them both a favor and offer up a topic of conversation. If nothing else, it would take their minds off what they were feeling.

"Nice car." She was happy that her offhand

remark sounded so sincere since her brain was in utter chaos with all the bells and whistles clanging in alarm as adrenaline and hormones surged through her body at dizzying speeds.

She saw the muscles in his shoulders visibly relax, distinct evidence that he was relieved that she wanted to snuff out—or at least ignore—the strong attraction hovering, thick and viscous as a heavy fog.

"Thanks," he murmured, not looking up.

She knew he was avoiding her eyes, avoiding her face. Avoiding the enticement that swirled around them under that tree. Her gaze riveted to his back. And she felt a deep disappointment when she realized that, rather than lessening the tension coiling inside her, seeing the tautness of his muscles release only heightened the visceral reactions. She wanted to reach out and run her fingertips across his bulky shoulders. But she was able to elude the urge. Just barely.

Mild panic set in, and she felt compelled to save herself, to save the both of them. From what, she hadn't a clue.

Stepping away from the car, away from *him*, she looked down the length of the shiny auto. She hadn't even noticed how it gleamed until now.

Before this moment, Jon had taken up every thought in her head. Well, maybe not every thought. A few of them had focused on Sydney. But now her breath left her in a gush of admiration.

"This isn't simply a nice car," she amended, awe unmistakable in her voice. "It's a *beautiful* car."

"Thanks," Jon said again. He tossed the spark plug gauge back into the toolbox, his upper body disappearing under the hood. "It's a '36 roadster. Sydney and I built it from the ground up."

The socket wrench clicked as Jon screwed the plug into place.

"Sydney helped you?"

"Mm-hmm," he said.

Studying the shiny, canary-yellow paint, she wryly commented, "I'd have taken you for a candy-apple-red kinda guy."

He chuckled. "Sydney picked out the color." He peered from around the hood and caught her gaze. "I did vote for red, actually. But Sydney talked me out of it." As they looked at each other, the mesmerizing attraction that charged the air made them self-conscious and his eyes shadowed over.

She blurted, "And Sydney actually helped you build it, huh?" Despite the massive, distracting awkwardness, Amber felt proud of her daughter.

"Yes," he told her, bending to work on the engine. "This is what takes up all our extra time. This is the reason why she doesn't play the flute. Or sing in the choir." His tone grew more muffled as he gruffly added, "Or take ballet lessons. Or bang on piano keys."

What was that she heard in his tone? Bitterness? Resentment? Regret? She was about to ask him when a young mechanic rounded the building, calling Jon's name.

"Yeah?" Immediately Jon reached for the ever present rag in his back pocket and began wiping off his fingers.

"The school nurse just called," he told Jon. "Sydney's sick. Upchucked her breakfast. She needs to come home."

Concern bit into Amber's brow, made her feel suddenly anxious. Her stomach felt jittery, as it did when she'd worked her stint in the ER. Only now, she couldn't seem to get the feeling under control. She couldn't seem to keep the shakiness at bay, or keep it from affecting her thought processes.

"Thanks, Dave," Jon said. "Can you hold down the fort until I get back?"

"Sure," the young man said.

Jon listed specific instructions regarding several

automobiles, but Amber was too intent on thoughts of Sydney to hear clearly.

The anxiety flooding her mind was... strange. Her career as a medical practitioner brought her into daily contact with sick people. But she never experienced this panicky apprehension that ate at her right now. Calm, cool logic was her best asset as a doctor. However, the distress she was feeling seemed nearly unmanageable. She *wanted* to pay attention to what Jon was saying, she *wanted* to find out more about what the school nurse might have said, but this frantic worry caught her in a grip she couldn't break.

Suddenly it came to her that this unfamiliar panic was stemming from her maternal side. Her mothering instincts. Up until this moment, Amber hadn't even realized she had any.

But then, she thought, wasn't it maternal concern that had her wanting Sydney to try hard to achieve great things in regards to her education? Of course, it was. And the pride she'd felt when Jon revealed that their daughter was actually helping him build this hot rod. That, too, was part of her motherly nature. This revelation was nice, but worry over Sydney crowded out everything else.

"Jon," she said.

He turned to face her.

"Is it all right if I go along with you?"

The question was weighted with a heavy layer of concern, and Jon evidently noticed it.

"Sure," he said. "Don't worry. She's okay. But I do need to get cleaned up just a little before we go. Let's go into my office and you can wait for me there."

As they rounded the building, Amber couldn't help but marvel at how relaxed he was. If he was worried about Sydney, he was hiding it pretty well.

"How can you be sure?" Her query slipped from her lips before she even had time to think about it. "That she's okay, I mean."

"If it was a real emergency," Jon said, entering one of the shop's big bay doors, "the principal would have called. And she wouldn't have passed a message through Dave. She'd have asked for me directly."

"Oh." There must have been curiosity in her tone, because he continued to elaborate how he knew the procedure.

"Sydney fell on the playground when she was in second grade," he told her. "She hit her head and had a pretty good gash that needed stitches, and that meant a trip to the emergency room." He grinned at her. "The principal called me."

Amber nodded, feeling a little more assured that Sydney wasn't too bad off.

"Besides," Jon continued, "I'm fairly sure I know what's wrong with her."

By this time, they were in his office, and she simply raised her brows and waited. He smiled at her, and every muscle in her body seemed to petrify at the sexy sight. The years had done nothing except make him more handsome than she could ever have imagined, and that was an incredible idea seeing as she'd felt he was simply to-die-for gorgeous when she'd been a teen. It became difficult to inhale, like all the oxygen in the air suddenly congealed into a thick, gelatinous mass.

"It's you."

There was no censure in his tone. But then she was too concerned with garnering control over her breathing and her erratic heartbeat caused by that too-charming grin of his to pay too much attention to the message being expressed in his words.

"I'm sure Sydney has turned herself inside out just thinking about meeting you today after school."

His smile widened and Amber was sure her

knees were going to fail her terribly and buckle under her. Shakily she eased herself down onto the armrest of the couch. Why did he have to be so darned good-looking? And why couldn't she seem to focus more of her energy on churning up those maternal worries?

It seemed that once Jon had assured her that Sydney was okay, that she wasn't in the throes of some violent illness, the motherly panic Amber had experienced had subsided and she'd become utterly transfixed by Jon's handsome face, his clear green gaze, and that seductive smile. That hum of attraction was back, full force.

"I think it will be best for Sydney—"

Jon continued to talk as though he was completely unaware of the effect he was having on her. For that, Amber was thankful.

"—if we got this first meeting over with between you two."

Her eyes were glued to his, and she couldn't seem to summon any sort of facial expression to save her soul. She was a mass of raw, pulsing nerves, aware of his every breath, his every move. All at once, he seemed to sense the tension she was feeling.

"Does that sound like a good idea to you?" His tone was soft, almost curious.

She couldn't get her tongue to form words, and she sat there feeling like a mute idiot.

"Amber?"

Speak, damn it! she silently commanded. Say something. Anything! Desperation built in the pit of her stomach, and she felt it roil there. It churned in a bubbling frenzy until it was strong enough to kick her into action.

"Sure." Her answer finally burst from her in a breathy whisper, and she prayed he didn't expect anything more from her at the moment.

"Great," he said. "Let me wash up and we'll take off."

Jon disappeared into the adjoining rest room and closed the door. Amber was only vaguely conscious of hearing water run as she berated herself for allowing this... this spellbinding force, or whatever it was called, to totally hypnotize her into this absolutely imbecilic, stupefied state. She had to snap out of it. She couldn't function like this. It was ridiculous.

Okay, so Jon was good-looking. So what? She had met good-looking men before. She had learned beside them, studied with them, worked with them, every day.

But none of them were Jon, a tiny voice silently pointed out.

Amber gulped air into her lungs. She stood up and paced to the window. She still felt a little shaky, but— she inhaled deeply again—she could ignore this attraction she was feeling. If she tried hard enough.

Water droplets glistened in his neatly combed hair, his hands and face freshly washed when he stepped from the rest room. He was drying his hands on a navy towel.

"I'm just about ready," he told her.

She tugged her long purse strap back up onto her shoulder. "Me, too," she said.

"Wait."

She froze as he approached her. He reached out and gingerly took her fingers away from the leather strap. His skin was warm and ever-so-slightly damp, and she detected the lemony aroma of soap.

"You're dirty," he said, gently wiping her fingertips with the towel. "That gauge you handed me must have been grimy. You'll get grease on your clothes if you're not careful."

He was so close. Too close. The lemon scent of

the soap couldn't hide the darkly sensuous aroma of his cologne, a fragrance that brought to mind hot, tropical nights spent in the arms of a lover.

She should step away from him, make it perfectly clear that she was quite capable of taking care of her own hygiene. But she didn't move. Didn't breathe.

"There," he said. "That's much better."

But he didn't release her fingers from his grasp. Helplessly her eyes were drawn to his face. The curve of his jaw, the slight crook of his nose that she knew had been caused by a particularly rough football tackle in high school, that green gaze that was intense with emotion.

It would be so easy to lean toward him. It would only take a tiny movement on her part, to give him the signal he seemed to be seeking. But she remained stubbornly still.

Finally he said, "Let's go. We'll take my car." And he started for the door.

Amber gave herself a moment. Waited a second or two for the haze in her head to clear.

You fool, her brain barked at her, *he wasn't looking for any signal. You're conjuring up a fine figment in that wild imagination of yours.*

But as she walked out into the shop, she knew in her heart that she wasn't a fool.

Chapter Six

The school building was the same one Amber had attended as an elementary student. The parking lot had been enlarged and new equipment had been added to the playground, but for the most part, not much more than that had changed over the years.

Jon hadn't said two words during the five-minute ride to the school. Awkwardness hovered, just waiting to swamp them. They were both doing their best to ignore it.

He paused at the door, allowing her to enter into the foyer first.

"Do you think she'll be in the principal's office?" Amber asked, her excitement over actually talking to Sydney mounting by the moment. "Or in the nurse's office?"

"When I've picked her up before," he said, "she was waiting in the... ah, there she is."

With a small tilt of his head, he indicated the school's main office to their immediate left. Her gaze followed his lead and came to rest on her daughter's pale face on the other side of the glass wall.

The poor child looked like an anxious bucket of nerves, her wide-eyed expression tearing at Amber's heart.

"She looks a wreck," she whispered to Jon.

"She's okay," he told her. "She looked the same way before her first roller-coaster ride." He chuckled softly. "In fact, that's the same expression she had *during* the ride, and for about an hour after, too."

Amber realized that he was attempting to allay the apprehension and worry she was feeling so strongly she was sure it must actually be emanating off her. But she knew nothing could calm her emotional state—nothing short of touching her daughter's face, discovering for herself that Sydney really was okay.

Glancing through the glass again, Amber saw that Sydney had become aware of her presence, the child's brown eyes growing large as they locked onto her.

"Come on," Jon told her. "Let's put her out of her misery."

Amber stopped short, his words striking her like an unexpected snakebite. "Misery?" Why would Jon think Sydney would feel miserable about meeting her?

"Yeah," he responded, "can't you see she's dying to meet you?"

"Oh—" she nodded "—I see." So he hadn't meant the statement hurtfully. Like a busy bee searching a pollen-coated flower, Amber's gaze lit on Sydney once again. Then she urged Jon forward. "I need to be put out of my misery, too." Her voice hushed to a whisper as she added, "Ten long years of misery."

She was only vaguely aware of the curious sidelong glance Jon cast her. But she didn't give it a thought because once she pushed open the office door and came face-to-face with Sydney, every nuance of her attention honed in on her daughter.

Standing there speechless, Amber felt the urge to kick herself. She had no idea what she should say. What *did* a mother say to a child she'd never met? Frustration only fanned the flames of anxiety burning in the pit of her stomach.

The perfect opening line was what she should have been pondering all morning rather than allowing so much of her energy to be sapped by the mysterious and hopeless attraction she'd felt toward Jon. Long moments seemed to tick by, even though Amber knew she'd only been in the office a few short seconds at the most. Why wasn't Jon stepping in to ease the discomfort laying heavy around them all? Ironically it was Sydney who spoke first, her tone hushed with obvious awe.

"You came."

Amber watched the child's bottom lip disappear between her teeth, astonishment clearly expressed in her wide, brown gaze.

"You really came."

A lump formed in Amber's throat. *Oh, please don't cry,* she silently pleaded with herself. *Please don't make an utter fool of yourself in front of this precious child.*

Unable to find the words to speak, and afraid of what her voice would sound like even if she did, Amber simply nodded, her eyes filling with happy tears as she, too, unwittingly captured her bottom lip between her teeth.

"I'll be taking my daughter home," Jon told the school secretary.

"Very good, Mr. Weston," the woman said, giving Amber a blatantly curious look. "Don't forget your backpack, Sydney."

After picking up her bag, Sydney lifted her hand to the secretary. "Bye, Mrs. Downham. See ya tomorrow."

"You take it easy this afternoon now." The woman addressed Sydney, but her gaze was still firmly affixed to Amber.

"I will," Sydney assured her.

Then the child did an extraordinary thing. She slipped her hand into Amber's and said, "Come on, Mom. Let's go."

Sydney's intention was obvious—to proudly and prominently reveal Amber's identity to the secretary. But Amber was so overwhelmed by hearing herself referred to as Mom, she didn't have enough of her wits about her to notice just how the elderly lady behind the big desk responded.

Mom. Her daughter had called her *Mom.* A brand-new lump of emotion welled in her throat, larger than the first. Amber found it hard to swallow, hard to breathe.

Sydney held on to her hand all the way out to

the car. Amber experienced a state of utter euphoria that was overwhelming. An elation that made her quite giddy. Made her actually see things in a new way. The trees surrounding the parking lot seemed to shimmer with life, their leaves a shocking and vibrant green. The clouds were larger, puffier, like huge tufts of marshmallow floating in a strikingly blue sky. And Amber knew that this new, resplendent vision was caused by the small, soft palm firmly nestled in hers.

Jon opened first the front passenger-side door of his car, and then the back one. "All aboard," he told them.

He smiled, but Amber noticed the tension on his face, in his voice, and her joyous fog parted long enough for her to wonder what he might be thinking. However, before Amber could come to any conclusions, her daughter graced her with a large-eyed, adoring expression that was enough to take away a person's breath.

"Can I sit up front with you?" Sydney asked her, pointing toward the bench seat of Jon's older model, fully restored Crown Victoria.

"Sure." Her answer was automatic. At that moment, she'd have agreed to ride up on top of the car's roof, if that's what her daughter would have wanted.

But what if Jon has rules about Sydney riding in the front seat? And what if there were state laws against it? The questions tramped across the happy haze of her brain, and she turned a querying gaze on Jon.

She tried to gauge if he might be feeling that she'd overstepped her bounds, but all she saw were the same tiny lines of strain bracketing his forced smile. Maybe that was why he seemed so tense. Maybe he was worried she might go overboard here.

I don't plan to come between you and Sydney. Her assurance to him reverberated in her head. His curt, cool response came close on its heels.

The last thing Amber wanted was for Jon to feel threatened. She glanced down at Sydney, "What I should have said was, you can sit up front if it's okay with your dad."

Jon glowered at her over their daughter's head.

Sure, the expression that passed his features seemed to say, let me be the bad guy.

Tossing him an apologetic look, Amber said to Sydney, "Maybe I ought to ride in the back."

"That would be the safer option," Jon said,

irritation flashing in his eyes as he slammed shut the front passenger door. "Would the two of you just get in already?"

Sydney hustled into the back seat and Amber quickly followed.

The ride home was filled with Sydney's chatter. Amber never guessed so many words could be spewed from a human mouth, so many different topics touched upon, in such a short amount of time. In the fifteen minutes it took for Jon to drive to his home, Amber found out a veritable fount of information about her daughter.

Sydney's teacher's name was Mrs. Edwards, and she was so nice she deserved to win Teacher of the Year. Apparently, Sydney's previous teacher had been the meanest witch of a teacher, a woman who had a terrible habit of tugging at her sagging stockings to the point that all the children in the school made fun of the ol' witch.

At this Jon had spoken Sydney's name in a tone of censure. Sydney had absently sang out a quick, "Sorry," and then continued down a different path.

April and Wendy, Amber learned, were Sydney's two best girlfriends, and Toby was her best boy friend. Not that Toby was her *boy*friend, Sydney took great pains to stress. He was just a friend who happened to be a boy. But he was still cool, even though most boys in her class sucked because they wouldn't let the girls play basketball with them on the playground. Sydney could make lots of baskets. Better than some of them, even. But Toby was okay, even though he sometimes played basketball with the other boys. Mrs. Edwards made history really fun. And she just gave the kids an awesome team assignment. They could make any kind of three-dimensional project they wanted. From history, of course. And Sydney had teamed up with Toby and the two of them were going to make a replica of King Tutankhamen's death mask.

Did Amber know that the real death mask was twenty-one inches high and was made of gold and lapis lazuli? Lapis lazuli was a beautiful blue mineral rock. She had learned that in science. Sydney didn't like science much. But last year, she and her dad had made a volcano that really erupted—an oh-so-cool oozy mixture of ketchup and sand—and she had won second place in the Science Olympiad. Next week Mrs. Edwards was taking the kids to the local orchard for a tour and Sydney was sure everyone would get to pick an apple. Right off the trees. At least that's what everyone thought was going to happen.

Jon pulled into his driveway. The brick ranch house sat back from the road. Big tulip trees shaded the wide front lawn, a stock-rail fence enclosed the even larger back yard.

"Nice," she murmured.

"Hey," Sydney continued to ramble, "maybe you'd like to come along."

Amber glanced down at the child. "Come along?"

"To the *orchard*. There are always a few parent chaperones when we go on trips. Bobby Taylor's mother always goes. Bobby's hyper and he's always gettin' into trouble. His mom comes so she can keep him under control. I could ask Mrs. Edwards tomorrow if there's room on the bus for you. I bet there is—"

"Whoa, now," Jon said as he cut the engine. "Slow down a little bit. You're overwhelming—"

He stopped, obviously stumped about something. Amber glanced at him curiously.

"—your mother."

The two words sounded stilted, stiff, and as uncomfortable as a brand-new shirt. Well, Amber decided, all of them were unaccustomed to the phrase. But she guessed they'd have to get used to using and hearing the words *Mom* and *Mother*.

After clearing his throat, Jon continued, "Let's get inside. You need to change out of your school clothes. We'll worry about the trip later."

Evidently Sydney's disappointment was sharp enough to silence her. At least for a moment or two.

They tramped around to the side of the house and entered through the door leading into the bright and airy eat-in kitchen.

"It's lovely," Amber exclaimed. "So open and welcoming."

"Thanks," Jon said.

"Dad built a lot of the house all by himself." Sydney's pride in her father was clearly evident in her voice, and Amber smiled.

"I woulda' helped," the child went on. "But a'course, I was too small back then."

Jon placed a loving hand on Sydney's shoulder. "You wield a wicked hammer," he said. "I'd have loved the help."

Sydney beamed under the compliment.

"Go on back to your room and change," Jon told her.

The child captured Amber's attention. "You wanna come see my room?"

Before Amber could respond, Jon said, "Don't

you think it would be best if you went and changed, and then made sure your room is picked up first?"

"Aw, Dad," Sydney complained. "I made my bed this morning."

"I know you did. But your pajamas were wadded in a ball on the floor by your dresser." Jon planted one hand on the back of a kitchen chair. "You should fold them up and put them away."

"I don't know why I gotta fold 'em up," she muttered. "I'm just gonna wear 'em again tonight."

Jon ignored her moaning. "And what about all those stuffed animals scattered about? Don't you want your mom to see your room when it's straightened up and not—"

"Okay, already," Sydney moaned, turning toward the hallway at the far end of the room.

Once they were alone, Jon turned to Amber. "Whoa," he said, "she gave up awfully easy."

Amber chuckled. "You presented a good argument."

Now it was his turn to laugh. "That's usually not enough with Sydney." He looked toward the empty hallway. "She must want to make a good impression on you."

His head swiveled, his gaze lighting once again

on Amber's face. The fatherly love she read in his eyes was appealing. Very much so. It was evident that Jon had a deep affection for Sydney, and that pleased Amber to no end.

"She's a good kid," he said.

Amber nodded. "I can tell." After a moment, she added, "You've done a good job of raising her." Then silence descended. And the good-humored camaraderie permeating the air began to metamorphose.

The change seemed to be excruciatingly slow. And torturously noticeable.

In an effort to avoid his green gaze, she lowered her eyes—and found herself admiring the corded muscles of his forearms, studying the pattern of the dark, springy hair growth on his tanned skin, noticing the strength of his long, tapering fingers, remembering how those fingers had brought her such exquisite pleasure.

The memory of one particular night came to her, sharp and clear. The air had been muggy, the temperature hot. In an effort to cool off, she and Jon had hopped on his motorcycle and sped out of town. He had taken her to Harrington Woods. The quiet isolation had been pure pleasure, the cool shade provided by the trees had been a relief. But it was what had taken place there beneath those towering trees, what Jon had done to her with his strong, yet gentle hands, that had her heart tripping in her chest, her breath turning shallow even now.

She closed her eyes against the graphic flashback. Swallowing, she shoved the erotic memories aside and steeled herself. Only then did she lift her gaze to his.

Her eyes widened. Jon looked just as disturbed as she felt, just as caught up in the past. Finally he blinked and then focused on her, his face taut. He truly seemed shaken. The thick mantle of mysterious attraction had settled on them yet again. To deny it would have been foolish, and futile.

"I have to go."

His voice was raw and grating. And Amber clamped her bottom lip between her teeth to keep from rushing to agree with him too quickly, knowing that to do so would have come off sounding extremely abrupt.

However, it was obvious that they both needed some space.

"I have loads of work to do at the shop," he continued. "You and Sydney have ten years to catch up on. And you don't need me here while you do that. I think Syd should be all right. You wouldn't mind if I went back to work, would you?"

Something in his tone gave her the impression he was arguing with himself: the father in him wanting to be close to his daughter should she need him during what could be an emotional experience, the man in him wanting desperately to run from the sensuous dynamite threatening to explode right under his feet. Amber easily empathized with him. She felt a strong urging to flee herself.

"I wouldn't mind at all," she quietly told him. But then she couldn't help pointing out the obvious. "But Sydney might mind. She might mind a lot. Seeing as how the two of us have never been alone before. I don't want her to feel awkward or self-conscious."

The moment was frozen in time, as Amber and Jon stared at each other in silence. How ironic that Amber would want Sydney to avoid the very discomfort she and Jon were facing right at this moment.

What you're feeling transcends awkwardness, surpasses self-consciousness, a voice rang in her head as loud as the peal of a bell. *What you're feeling is a drawing, a pulling, a gravitation.*

Allure. Temptation. Beguilement.

Strong words, Amber realized. Powerful feelings. Feelings that were, at this very moment, putting up one heck of a battle inside her.

"Right," he said, looking around frantically for his best escape route. "You're absolutely right. I'll go talk to her."

With that said, he made a hasty retreat down the hallway and turned the corner out of sight.

Amber set her purse on the oak table and moved to the green-tiled island. She smoothed her fingers across the cool surface. A diversion was what she needed. Something that would take her mind off Jon and the heady sensations that swirled around them when they were together.

Glancing around her, she decided this really was a lovely room. A kitchen a woman would enjoy cooking in, entertaining in, planning meals that would lovingly nourish her happy family.

Her chin tipped up, and she felt a frown bite deeply into her brow. Where had that thought come from? she wondered. She wasn't one to think about hearth and home. When Jon had rejected her, and then only months later she'd lost her child, Amber had pretty much decided having a family wasn't for her. The decision hadn't been a conscious one—she'd just resolved that love simply hurt too much. So she'd locked up her heart. And focused on her studies. Consequently she had been a damn good medical student, graduating in the top ten percent of her class. She could have specialized, gone on to study, in-depth, any number of areas in the medical field. But she'd wanted to become a general M.D. Someone who looked after families...

The thought trailed off as questions seeped into her brain. Why had she chosen to become a *family* practitioner? Was it because she'd shut out of her life any idea of having a husband and children of her own? Had she chosen her profession—caring for parents and their offspring—in some attempt to fill some kind of void inside her?

The questions were daunting.

Jon barreled back into the room, pulling his keys from his pocket as he came.

"Everything's all set," he told her.

Amber couldn't help but notice how he was avoiding eye contact with her.

"Sydney's more than happy to stay here with

you." He moved to the back door. "I'll be home a little after six, if that's okay."

Amber told him that was fine. He opened the door, and then turned back as an idea struck him.

"If you'll give me your keys," he said, "I'll have Dave drive your car over here. One of the other mechanics will follow him to bring him back to the shop. That way your car will be here if you need it."

"That would be great," she said. She went to the table, and when she reached for her purse to get her fob, Jon actually took a backward step.

She found the key ring and he took it, wordlessly, a myriad of cryptic messages expressed in his gaze. Then after giving her a quick nod, he was gone.

What the two of them were experiencing—attraction, allure, temptation—was simply too obvious to be ignored for very long. She'd tried to disregard the feelings, as she was sure Jon had. But brushing it aside wasn't quashing it. This magnetism just seemed to grow stronger. Their feelings were going to have to be acknowledged. Talked about. Reckoned with.

Maybe by bringing it out into the open, discussing it like two mature adults, the emotions could be put to rest.

But that would have to be left for some other time. For now, Amber needed to give her daughter her undivided attention.

* * *

Over the next three afternoons, Amber got a taste of what she imagined heaven must be like, and she was finding the experience to be utterly delectable. From three o'clock until six o'clock, she discovered what it meant to be a mom. Feelings blossomed inside her—maternal sentiments she'd never experienced before coming home to Pine Meadow, before meeting her adorable, fun-loving, outgoing daughter. Feelings that were warm and fuzzy and... completely indescribable. If some scientist could isolate whatever chemical the brain secreted that conjured these complicated feelings—this joyous euphoria, this giddy pleasure, this intense pride—and bottle the stuff, he'd become a millionaire overnight.

Sydney was intelligent and quick-witted. A joy to be around. And Amber savored those three hours she spent with her daughter every afternoon. Amber would meet Sydney at the bus stop and walk with her back to Jon's house. Usually

Jon picked up Sydney and took her to the shop, but he'd agreed to allow Amber to stay with their daughter until he arrived home from work.

That very first evening, the day that she had gone to school with Jon to pick up Sydney, Amber had stayed and had dinner with the two of them. With disastrous results. The air was so awkward between Amber and Jon that Sydney had picked up on it. Misreading the tense emotions vibrating in the air as anger, Sydney had asked why her parents were upset with each other. Jon had done his best to calm her fears, but if it hadn't been for Sydney's endless chatter, the meal would have been eaten in total silence.

Amber tried to snuff out the electricity that pulsed between her and Jon, but she failed. Miserably. She knew they needed to talk about what was happening to them. And she was certain that once they did, once they acknowledged these echoes from their past attraction—at least that's how she'd come to describe what she was feeling for Jon—then they could both put all this silliness behind them. However, a private talk with Jon was next to impossible with Sydney at Amber's elbow every moment. So after that first evening, Amber avoided further discontent, making sure she came up with some plausible excuse, and left the house as soon as Jon arrived home from work around six-fifteen. But getting their feelings out in the open was inevitable.

However this Friday afternoon, Amber found herself driving down a lonely road rather than spending a few delightful hours with her daughter. Seems that Sydney had to get together with Toby to work on their history project, the replica of King Tut's death mask. Although Sydney was disappointed that she and Amber wouldn't have the afternoon together, Amber had also heard an underlying excitement in her daughter's voice about the project when she'd called about the change of plans.

Amber slowed to a stop at a crossroads and smiled. Sydney had gotten off the subject at hand during their phone conversation. As usual, Amber thought, her grin widening. Sydney had told her that Toby lived on the outskirts of Harrington Woods, and then she had launched into a detailed discourse describing the fort she and Toby were building in one particular tree. Of course, Sydney had gone on, they wouldn't have time to work on that this evening, not with their project due the middle of next week.

It was this discussion that got Amber to thinking. About Harrington Woods. About these whispers from the past that were pulling at her every single time she was with Jon. If she were to face the past, confront the strong attraction—the powerful love—she'd felt for Jon, then maybe she would be better able to deal with what she was feeling for him in the here and now. And what better place for such a confrontation than the spot in Harrington Woods that all those years ago they had deemed "theirs"?

No better place, she'd decided, pulling onto the shoulder of the two-lane road when she spied the overgrown dirt lane she knew had been her and Jon's "entrance into Paradise."

"This isn't Harrington Woods," she remembered whispering into Jon's ear one hot, sultry afternoon, "this is paradise." And from that day on, their spot had been dubbed Paradise.

It was nothing more than a dirt track now with scrub brush and sticker bushes standing sentinel, reaching out to snag anyone who might trespass. She didn't dare risk scratching the paint job on her car by driving down the lane. So she switched off the engine, locked the car door and carefully picked her way through the narrow opening into the woods.

Silence enveloped her. And with each step she took down the hard-packed trail, the outside world seemed to slip farther and farther away. Isolation. Solitude. Those were the very things she and Jon had sought in coming here. Not complete isolation, of course, but seclusion for the two of them away from the rest of life. And they had found that. Time and again. Here, in this place.

It was so easy to imagine herself at sixteen and seventeen. It was so easy to conjure what she'd thought were long lost feelings of eager anticipation of being with the boy she loved. She could almost feel the wind against her skin as she rode behind Jon on his motorcycle. The smell of his leather jacket, pungent and heady. The strength of his broad back and thighs as she snuggled close to him, holding on tight while they bumped down the lane toward Paradise. Every nerve ending in her body alert with tingling expectation and impatience to taste his kiss, feel his hands on her skin. Because she knew with joyous certainty that, after talking and teasing and laughing together, they would express their love in a most physical and intimate manner.

Amber stopped, and smiled when she found it. Paradise had changed. Just as the lane into the Harrington Woods had become overgrown, so had Paradise. But the felled tree that had served as a seat was still there, covered with moss and lichen now. As were the initials Jon had lovingly carved into the bark of a nearby oak. The letters had become a little distorted by the tree's growth over the years, but Amber could easily read them.

Sighing, she simply stood there and enjoyed the serenity; the vibrant greens in so many different shades, the rustling of the slight breeze through the leaves overhead, the scurrying of some unseen squirrel or chipmunk. She blinked, turning her head to look toward where she'd come from, when a different sound broke the tranquil atmosphere—

The distinct *pug, pug, pug* of an approaching motorcycle.

Chapter Seven

She should have panicked when he appeared on the trail. She should have gasped. Or experienced embarrassment at having been caught seeking out this place. The least she should have been surprised. But she wasn't any of these things. In fact, his showing up here—*now*—in Paradise seemed to be the most natural thing in the world.

He cut the engine, pulled off his helmet, ran his fingers through his dark hair. Amber did the only thing she could do—she offered him a welcoming smile. A smile he returned. And immediately she was aware that every bit of the stifling awkwardness she had felt between them since she'd returned to Pine Meadow was gone. Dissolved into thin air.

Amber knew without any doubt that the

location was the cause. Paradise was, simply put, a magical place. A place where nothing bad could ever happen. A place where dreams came to fruition. A place of unending happiness... no matter what might be happening "out there" in the real world.

"Hi," she said.

His soft smile widened in silent greeting.

"I dropped Sydney off at Toby's and saw your car parked along the side road," he said, explaining his presence.

But Amber chose to believe that it was fate that brought him here. That enchanted explanation fitted the moment much better. At least, it did in her mind.

"I was headed back to the shop," he told her. "But then..." He expelled a short, quick exhalation that was filled with irony. "It was almost as if my bike was headed down the path before I even had a chance to think about turning."

This admission only added to the mystical quality of the moment, only increased her certainty that destiny had stepped into this situation.

Jon lowered the kickstand and lifted himself off

the motorcycle. Then he set his helmet on the black leather seat.

"It's been a long time," he said as he approached her.

Watching him gaze across Paradise, Amber sensed the awe building inside him, saw the memories churning in his head through the windows of his clear, green eyes. She understood completely, because she felt awed herself.

"Yes" was all she said, the overwhelming mesmerism of the situation, of the place, forcing her voice to a mere whisper.

His tone, too, was hushed, when, after a moment, he said, "What would have possessed us to—"

His sentence was cut short, his face actually tingeing with embarrassed color. Amber shook her head, unable to stop the disconcerted grin that pulled and then lingered at one corner of her mouth. She knew exactly what he was thinking. To what he was referring. In a moment of boldness, she decided to finish his thought.

"Strip down naked in the wide-open spaces of Harrington Woods?" she supplied.

They looked at each other in total silence. And

then finally they burst out laughing until they were both teary-eyed.

"Teenagers can be very..." This time she was the one finding it difficult to voice what was on her mind.

"Uninhibited?" he offered.

Again they shared a chuckle, this one smaller, less sheepish and more intimate.

She looked around at the trails. "It's a wonder we weren't ever, ah, interrupted. By hikers, or people out looking for a quiet picnic spot. Or the park ranger, even. We were awfully lucky, wouldn't you say?"

"Well, we were either very lucky," he said, "Or we were someone's erotic entertainment."

Amber gasped, horrified by the mere idea of being spied upon in compromising circumstances. "Don't say that!"

Jon laughed at her. But she wasn't upset. The humor glittering in his eye was darned appealing.

Suddenly he fell silent. Then he said, "Wow, would you look at that."

He studied their initials in the oak tree.

"Yes—" Amber went to the tree, reached up and traced the letters with her fingertip "—it's still here after all these years." She smiled softly, not feeling the least bit self-conscious as she read, "JW loves AH 4-ever."

Before she realized it, he'd come up behind her. So close, she could feel his warm breath brush the side of her face, feel the solid mass of his body, not touching her, but only a fraction of an inch away.

She'd meant to come to Harrington Woods to face the demons of her past. To confront the bygone love she'd felt for Jon, so that she could put to rest this silly attraction she felt for him in the present. But at this moment, in this place, the hypnotic allure that enthralled her seemed anything but silly. It seemed real. It seemed honest. It *was* honest; and had little to do with the past.

"It was true, you know," he said against her ear. He placed his hand on her shoulder. "I loved you with every fiber of my being."

The magnitude of this confession wasn't lost on her. When most young men his age—eighteen and nineteen years old—had been driven by their hormones to see just how many girls they could score, Jon had pledged himself to her. Wholly. Completely.

"I know." She closed her eyes. Reveled in the heated male scent of him. Relished the feel of his touch. Marveled at how the very air seemed to come alive all around them.

Amber recognized his affirmation was offered as a means to assure her of his feelings at the time they had made love as teens here. She'd been aware of his feelings then.

"I know you did," she repeated.

She turned to face him and then leaned her back against the rough bark of the oak, instinctively knowing he would close the gap between them. And he did.

"I never doubted it," she said, gazing into his gorgeous emerald eyes. Those eyes that had always had such power over her.

Her last statement wasn't the complete truth. In the end she had doubted him. With very good reason. But now wasn't the time to remember old hurts, it was a time to reminisce about—*to give tribute to*—all the wonderful times they had shared together. And there had been many.

He stroked the length of her cheek with the back of his index finger, his touch feather light, and Amber surrendered to the urge to tilt her head and close her eyes. And then she did the most incredible thing. She reached up, took his hand in both of hers and pressed the backs of his fingers to her lips. And with his hand still captured in hers, she opened her eyes and stared directly into his.

She paused, waiting to be swamped by a wave of embarrassment. And when it didn't come, she suspected that was due to Jon's reaction to her startlingly sensuous behavior. From the look in his eyes, one would be led to believe that what she'd done was utterly normal. Completely natural and expected.

He leaned close, his nose lightly brushing her jaw, and then her cheekbone, as he slid his fingers around her delicate throat. It wasn't a threatening motion in any way. No, it was more like he needed to feel her bare flesh against his, and her neck was all that was available to him. Instinctively her hands went to his shirtfront, her fingers splaying across the broad expanse of his chest. Lord, he felt so good, so strong, under her palms.

"You've become quite a woman, Amber," he whispered. "The years have made you... beautiful."

His compliment made her shy. The passing years had changed her. And she was never more conscious of the changes as she was right now. The faint lines fanning the corners of her eyes, the laugh lines bracketing her mouth, the extra weight on her hips. Beautiful was not a word she'd use to describe herself. But hearing him call her that made her feel... as tingly as a teenager on her first real date.

"So beautiful," he murmured against her ear.

Her body seemed to rouse from some kind of coma—as if it had been forced into some magical sleep and was being reawakened after many long years. Her heart pounded. Her blood pulsed. Her stomach danced. Her nerves prickled. Every inch of her skin was alert and waiting. Waiting for his touch. His kiss.

He pressed his nose into her hair and then against her neck, and she could hear him inhale gently, slowly, fully.

"You *smell* beautiful."

His palms smoothed over her shoulders and down her arms, lightly grazed the sides of her elbows, the backs of her fingers, all the way down to the very tips. Finally he settled his hands snugly on her hips.

"You *feel* beautiful."

A heady need sprouted to life within her. Desire that took root in the form of a warm pulse deep inside the very core of her being. Her throat felt so dry that it ached. All she wanted was to feel his hands on her bare skin again, feel his mouth against hers.

Lifting his head, he looked into her eyes. "You *look* beautiful."

The hunger in his gaze fed her growing passion until it throbbed with scorching heat.

Amber realized there remained one relevant sensation on which he could comment—*the sense of taste*. Lord, if he didn't kiss her this very moment, she'd go insane.

As if reading her thoughts, he lowered his head and planted on her lips the lightest of kisses. He gave one corner of her mouth an identical butterfly-kiss, then gifted the other corner with yet another.

Like the rapid growth of a leafy vine, the need in her curled with delicious heat, extending itself into every nook, every cranny inside her, until the hot pulsation was her only focus, her only concern.

Nourishing this uncontrollable hunger became a sudden, monumental obsession. Jon's gossamer kisses were nice, tantalizingly so, but they were nowhere near substantial enough to satisfy the immense desire his nearness, his touch, conjured in her.

"Honey sweet," he said, the obvious desire he

felt ripping his tone into jagged edges. "Delicious. Even better than I remember."

How would he know? she wondered almost sulkily. How could he know what she tasted like when his mouth had barely brushed hers? What he needed was a *real* kiss, she decided. Some sultry, steamy contact that would leave no doubt in his mind as to what she tasted like.

She lifted her hands, framed his face with them, and said, "Here." And then more urgently, "Really kiss me."

Her assertiveness evidently surprised him, for his eyes widened a fraction when she spoke. But she didn't dwell on his reaction for long, the craving inside her forcing her to act, and she drew his mouth to hers.

His lips were firm and warm and moist, and she ran her tongue across them, ever so lightly, in a silent request for entry. A request he granted.

She slid her arms around his body, up along the hard muscles of his back, and hugged him to her. Her nipples budded to life, hard as stone, as her breasts were crushed against his chest.

Their tongues danced, languidly. Hands smoothed. Fingers kneaded. Muscles bunched. And relaxed.

The sound of their breathing became audible, even frantic, as their heightened excitement caused their hearts to pound furiously, caused their bodies to demand more oxygen. She heard his jagged inhalations, and she found the sound so erogenous that the need in her grew ever more insatiable.

Skin. She had to feel his bare flesh against hers. Now.

Mindlessly she tugged the tail of his shirt from where it had been tucked in the waistband of his jeans. Reaching beneath it, she placed the flat of both hands against his bare back and slowly roved.

His kiss wandered then, from her lips, to her jaw, to her neck. He kissed the length of it, down, and then up again, nipping the edge of her jaw between his teeth.

"You taste like heaven."

There was something in his voice, some delirious quality she heard, that made her smile with deep satisfaction and a pleasure that was so pure she felt it all the way to the tips of her toes. She dragged her hands around his waist, settling them under his shirtfront on the rippled hills and valleys of his taut stomach muscles. His breath caught sexily, and he reached to press his palm against the back of her hand, the fabric of his clothing a thin, separating barrier.

"You keep touching me like this," he said, his voice scratchy with emotion, "and you're going to drive me crazy."

Amber was amazed that their thoughts were so in tune. Her languid smile widened, and their gazes locked.

Apparently he took her silent response as some sort of invitation, for he ever so slowly reached for the bottommost button of her blouse. He released it, and then moved to the next, never breaking eye contact with her.

Amber thought her heart couldn't possibly beat any faster, nor her blood pump any hotter, but the mere anticipation of feeling his hands on her body sent her entire system into chaotic overdrive. Her breathing became as rough as his. Her knees went wobbly and she was relieved to have the solid old oak tree behind her for support.

Only when he'd unfastened the final button and gently folded back the facings of her blouse did his eyes stray from hers. His gaze lowered with excruciating slowness to her chest, and she watched as longing darkened his eyes to a deep hunter green.

He whispered her name and at the same time slid his hands under her breasts, capturing the weight of them in his palms. She felt the warmth of his skin through the lacy fabric of her flesh-colored bra and thought that surely she would faint dead away from the sheer pleasure of his touch. Leaning her head back against the oak tree, she closed her eyes and basked in the heat of the passionate fire he stirred in her.

She sensed him lowering his head, felt him press a hot, wet kiss on her breast, and she could no more have suppressed the gasp that escaped her than she could have stopped the change of the seasons or the rising of the sun and moon. He leaned forward, his thighs on her thighs, and he exhaled, grinding his hips into her. The hot hardness of him pressed against her lower abdomen and Amber curled her fingers, gently raking her nails up the length of his back.

His spine arched and again he murmured her name. Then he crushed his mouth against hers in a kiss that bordered on savage. But it was just what Amber wanted. Just what she needed.

Their fingers became frantic as they plucked at each other's clothing; Amber trying to unbutton his shirt, he trying to unfasten her bra and slide it and her blouse off her shoulders.

A horn sounded. A loud horn. The horn of a huge sixteen-wheeler.

Jon and Amber both started, their heads turning toward the direction of the highway, their hands still, their eyes wide with astonishment. But all they saw were green trees in the late afternoon, all they heard were birds singing overhead. They looked at one another. Stared in silence. Searched each other's hungry-yet-uncertain gazes. Jon was the first to break the silence.

"There was a time," he said, "when we'd never have let the sounds of traffic stop us."

"I remember." She tried hard to hold on to the delectable haze swarming around them, a sensuous fog she was reluctant to disturb.

"I guess the years have made us a little more self-conscious."

She had to smile. "A little more inhibited?"

It was a rhetorical question, as he evidently understood.

His hands slid to her waist, and after a long silence, he asked, "What are we doing, Amber?"

She rolled her eyelids closed. If he wasn't careful, his words were going to dissolve the sexy vapor that enveloped them, the way the sun burned off the haze of morning. She drew her bottom lip between her teeth for a moment, then opened her eyes to look at him. "I don't know. I don't want to think about it."

"Don't you think we should?"

Questions. Why was he asking such complicated questions? Couldn't he just enjoy the moment? Couldn't he just allow them to get caught up in the magic of this place?

They *had* gotten caught up in the magic of Paradise, she realized. *And they shouldn't have.* The thought was like a dash of icy water on hot skin.

She shifted her weight, and he stepped away from her. Immediately she comprehended the enormous mistake she'd just missed making, and the person with whom she'd just missed making it.

Amber would have made love right here on the ground. Among the weeds, the undergrowth, the poison ivy. No questions asked. She'd have given her body to Jon. A man she didn't even know, really. A man she suspected of robbing her of the most important thing in a woman's life... her child.

What the hell was the matter with her? How could she have let sexual desire override logical thinking? It was ludicrous. It was inexcusable.

"You're right," she murmured, suddenly unable to look him in the face as she fumbled to dress herself. "Absolutely right."

Absently he stuffed his shirttail into his jeans. "We need to talk about this, Amber."

"I know we do. But not right now." The mere suggestion of talking about what had just taken place between them mortified her.

"But don't you think now would be the perfect time—"

"Please, Jon. Can't you see I'm... *embarrassed?*"

He frowned. His voice was gentle as he said, "But you're not the only one to blame here. I'm just as much an adult as you. I let things get out of hand, too. I made a conscious decision to—"

"Not now!" she begged. Then she whispered, *"Please."*

She turned her back on him, flattening her hand against the rough bark of the tree, wishing she could just disappear.

Dr. Amber Holloway, educated woman, medical practitioner, unable to control her libido. Unable to restrain her sexual cravings for a man who might have done her horribly wrong. She was ashamed of herself. Ashamed of her behavior.

"We'll talk," she promised. "Some other time. I

need to be alone right now. I need to get myself under control."

He sighed, but he said nothing more.

After a moment, she heard him move away from her, heard him strap on his helmet, heard the engine of his bike roar to life. And soon, the sound of his motorcycle was disappearing down the trail.

Amber looked down the length of her; the buttons of her blouse fastened wrong, the fabric wrinkled, her flesh still clamoring with lust. She felt totally betrayed. Not by Jon. But by her own body. She closed her eyes, clenched her fists, hung her head, and silently berated herself with all manner of wicked words.

* * *

Amber pulled into Jon's driveway, grinning at how her daughter danced a merry jig and waved a hearty hello at her. She'd accepted Sydney's invitation to a Saturday afternoon picnic even though she felt more than a small twinge of trepidation over seeing Jon for the first time since they had shared a kiss in the woods.

Really, she silently scolded herself, *don't you think what the two of you shared was a little more than a kiss?*

What with both of you so ardent in your passions? So disheveled in body and mind when the episode was cut short?

Ignoring the irritating questions, Amber called out a greeting to her daughter as she exited her car.

"Cake!" Sydney squealed with glee.

"It's not homemade," Amber apologized. "I bought it. My hotel room didn't come equipped with a kitchen."

"Mmm, coconut," her daughter remarked, leaning close to sniff the confection. "Chocolate's my favorite. But coconut runs a close second."

Amber smiled warmly. "Good. I'm glad my contribution to lunch will be appreciated."

"Oh, yes. Yummy!" Then Sydney trotted over to where her dad was working on the yellow roadster under the shade tree. "Dad and I took Bessie out for a ride this morning," she said to Amber. "And now we're giving her a good wax job."

"Ah," Amber said, very aware that Jon hadn't greeted her, that he hadn't even looked up, "so the car has a name."

"Yep," Sydney said. "And I christened her, didn't I, Dad?"

Only when Jon had been addressed directly did he stop rubbing the car's hood in a circular motion.

He straightened his spine, turned his eyes on his daughter. "You sure did," he said.

"Mom brought a cake," Sydney announced.

Amber nearly smiled at the unspoken admonishment in her daughter's tone. Sydney seemed to be urging her father to use better manners.

"I see," Jon said. "It looks good. Delicious."

Their gazes caught and held when he spoke. Amber immediately remembered that he'd used that very word just yesterday when he'd described how she tasted to him. She felt her face flame.

Jon then addressed Sydney. "Why don't you take the cake inside? Put it on the counter in the kitchen."

"Okay."

Sydney took the cake from her mother and trooped toward the side door of the house.

"You're late," Jon said when their daughter was out of earshot. "I was beginning to think you weren't coming. I was afraid Sydney was going to be disappointed."

"I'd never disappoint Sydney," she said.

No matter how awkward things are between us. The unspoken words hung heavy in the air.

Jon finally said, "Good. I'm glad to hear you say that."

His tone, along with his accusation, sent Amber into defensive mode.

"I'm late because I stopped at the bakery in town," she told him. "They were busy. And then I had a hard time deciding what I should bring."

"Well," he commented levelly, "you made a perfect choice. Like Sydney said, she loves coconut. So do I."

I didn't bring it for you. The snippy retort was on the tip of her tongue, but she restrained herself. Because it would have been a bold-faced lie. Yes, she had hoped her daughter would like the dessert she'd chosen, but she couldn't deny the fact that she'd remembered Jon's love of coconut cake.

Once again, her darned emotions started to churn. Insulted by his suggestion that she might disappoint Sydney, and now she felt pleased by his compliment. Lord, the man wasn't happy unless he had her feelings twisted in knots.

Inadvertently her gaze dropped to his chest, to the three buttons of his cotton Henley... three unfastened buttons that exposed a small V of springy, dark chest hair. She realized this was the first time she'd seen him in anything other than his blue uniform shirt. He looked good. Very good.

Dragging her gaze back to his, she parted her lips and sucked in a short, silent breath when she saw the expression on his handsome face. He knew! He knew she found him attractive.

Don't be a moron! her brain raged. Of course, he knew. How could he not, after that steamy kiss you laid on him yesterday?

Annoyance at herself puffed up inside her. How could she be attracted to a man who most probably betrayed her? She had to tell him. Today. That nothing like that... that sexy episode in Paradise could ever happen again.

The atmosphere on that bright autumn day grew more ungainly by the moment. Amber opened her mouth to speak, but at that moment Sydney came bursting outside.

"So—" Sydney started talking before she was even halfway across the lawn "—what do you think of Bessie? Isn't she great?"

Amber nodded enthusiastically. "She sure is. Your dad told me that you helped build the car."

"I did." Sydney's chest puffed with pride. "Dad let me make lots of decisions about Bessie, too. It was my idea to have wide whites all around."

"Wide whites?"

"The tires," Jon explained. "'Wide whites' means the tires have extra-wide whitewalls."

Amber noticed how little of the outside walls of the tires were black. The tires were different from any she'd seen before. But then, she wasn't in the habit of inspecting hot rods up close, either.

"And 'all around' means all the way around the car," Sydney piped up. "As in all four tires as opposed to just the front two."

"Ah, I see," Amber said. "They really are sharp looking."

Sydney's smile was nothing less than glorious. "Thanks. But the best part is the engine. It's a 454 BBC crate motor with a huffer and NOS injection." Hearing the technical jargon spewing from her ten-year-old daughter had Amber's eyes widening in surprise. Looking over to Jon, Amber said, "Could you explain all that in layman's terms for me?"

Jon's green eyes glittered with merriment. "A 454, as in cubic inches. *BBC* stands for Big Block Chevrolet. And *crate* means the motor was factory-produced and shipped in a crate."

"Ah..." Amber nodded. "That one is easy enough to understand."

He grinned. "Huffer means the engine has a supercharger that compresses the fuel and air mixture. It produces more horsepower. And the NOS is a system that sprays nitrous-oxide gas into the intake of the engine. Again, for more horsepower."

Meaning to impress Sydney with what little she did know about cars, Amber pointed to the tailpipe and commented, "Bessie's got dual exhaust."

"Actually," Sydney said, "the exhaust system is set up with block hugger SS headers running into—"

"Okay, okay." Amber laughed. "Enough of the technical stuff. It's a foreign language to me. But I guess it all adds up to speed, right?" She looked at Jon. "Bessie goes fast."

"In the easiest of layman's terms, yes," Jon said, and then he laughed.

The sound of his laughter made her heart hitch behind her ribs. She wished she had a logical explanation for her attraction to this man. She'd have thought that after all these years his appeal to her would have waned. But as she stood there, her palms clammy, her pulse racing as fast as Bessie's state-of-the-art engine from simply listening to him laugh, Amber knew the opposite was the truth.

As usual, Sydney's gears shifted swiftly when she changed the topic of the conversation by saying, "Ya gotta come inside. To my room. I want you to see the death mask."

Excitement gleamed in Sydney's brown eyes, and seeing it was enough to erase all the confusion swimming around in Amber's head.

"Me and Toby are almost done," Sydney said.

"Toby and I are almost finished." Jon's correction came automatically.

The child glanced up at her father's face, confusion knitting her brow as she shrugged. "That's what I said."

Jon's brows shot up wryly. "Not quite."

Amber chuckled. "I'd love to see the mask, honey. But maybe your dad needs help preparing lunch."

"I'm almost finished here," Jon said, indicating the polish job he was giving the car. "And then I'll fire up the grill. I thought we'd enjoy the weather and eat outside."

"That would be nice," Amber responded.

"It'll be thirty minutes or so before the coals are

ready," he continued. "You and Sydney can spend some time together."

Sydney took Amber by the hand. "Come on, Mom," she said, tugging Amber toward the house.

"I'm coming, I'm coming." Amber laughed. "Impatient little thing, aren't you?"

She marveled at how Sydney could turn the gray clouds of her emotions into bright, sunny thoughts. She loved this child. Couldn't believe she'd actually given birth to this lovely and lively creation. Amber felt truly blessed.

Sydney's room would have been the dream of any little girl. The four-poster bed with its frilly pink canopy. The white dresser, bookcase and desk, all matching. The pink curtains that matched the canopy and the bedspread. Even the carpet was pink. The whole room was feminine. Almost too much so. It simply didn't seem to fit her daughter's character, what with Sydney's love of cars and sports, and her abhorrence of dresses, or anything dainty or lacy, for that matter.

On her first visit into her daughter's room, Amber had found out that this furniture, the bedspread and curtains, had been a gift for Sydney on her eighth birthday.

A gift from her grandmother. Helen Weston.

Sydney had been excited about the prospect of having her room redecorated. But then, without even asking Sydney, Helen had all this white furniture delivered. Sydney hated her room. She'd wanted bunk beds, not a stupid, frilly canopy. But Jon had scolded her and told her that she shouldn't be ungrateful. He didn't want her to hurt her grandmother's feelings. So the furniture stayed.

"Here it is," Sydney said.

The mask was large. A full-size replica of Tutankhamen's death mask. The plaster had been painstakingly hand-molded. It was by no means perfect, but the Egyptian face was certainly discernible. The plaster had been spray-painted with gold paint, and Sydney was in the process of adding deep blue paint that obviously represented the lapis on the real mask.

"It's amazing," Amber said. "You and Toby are doing a great job."

"Toby's coming tomorrow so we can finish it," Sydney told her. "It's due on Monday."

Then Sydney launched into a long story explaining why Toby couldn't come today. That his grandmother was in a nursing home and he had to drive a kabillion miles to visit her.

The room grew quiet suddenly, and Amber

glanced at her daughter. Sydney was fidgeting with the end of her belt, the tiny tail dangling from the buckle. Something was obviously on the child's mind, and Amber thought she knew what was about to happen.

Up until this moment, all her time with her daughter had been spent talking about Sydney; her thoughts and feelings about school, her friends and teachers, her favorite things to do, to see, to wear, to eat. Amber had spent days learning everything there was to know about her daughter. And she'd loved every minute of it.

Amber had been content to let the child ramble from one subject to the next in her jubilant attempt to cram as much information as she could into their talks. But Amber knew Sydney must be curious about her. The only information the child had gleaned was that Amber lived in Connecticut and was a doctor. Sydney must want to know what her mother has been doing all these years, and why she hadn't been in Pine Meadow.

Those were questions she read in Sydney's shadowed gaze—questions Amber was more than happy to answer.

Chapter Eight

"How long will you be staying?"

Sydney's voice was so tentative and shy, it ripped at Amber's heart.

"Today?" Amber asked. "Why, I'll stay as long as you like, sweetheart."

"No, I mean..." Again, the child's whole body went timid. "I mean in town. How long will you be staying in Pine Meadow?"

"Oh, honey," Amber said, wrapping her arm lovingly around Sydney's shoulder. "I don't want you to worry. Everything's going to work out fine. I won't let us lose touch again."

One corner of Sydney's mouth tipped up endearingly. "I like that."

Amber's brows raised in inquiry.

Sydney's eyes averted. "I like it when you call me those names. You know, sweetheart and honey."

Squeezing her tight, Amber said, "Well, you are my sweetheart. And my honey."

She giggled, hugging her mom around the waist, burying her face in Amber's stomach. Amber went all warm and quivery inside, and the love she felt seemed to expand and grow, as if her heart was a big balloon filling with more and more fuzzy emotion. The feeling was so intense it almost hurt, but it was the nicest kind of pain.

The edge of the mattress compressed as Amber sat down.

"I don't really know how long I'm staying," she continued quietly, honestly.

The idea of leaving Sydney behind while she went back up north to continue in her new medical practice was upsetting to Amber. She hadn't really thought about it until this very moment.

"But you can bet," she said, "I won't leave without saying goodbye, or giving you many different ways to contact me—my address, my work number, my email address. You already have my cell number. I imagine you'll be visiting me up in Connecticut if your dad says it's okay."

"Ya mean it?" Sydney's eyes lit up.

Amber nodded, chuckling. "I mean it. If your dad agrees."

"Oh, he'll let me come," the child said. "If he says no I'll just pitch a hissy fit until he gives in." Then her voice took on a low, conspiratorial tone. "That's how I get my way."

The smile on Amber's mouth faded. She couldn't believe what she was hearing. Granted, she hadn't knowingly been a parent for very long, but logic alone dictated that Sydney needed to be called down for her manipulative manner. A scheming attitude simply wasn't fitting.

Yes, her daughter's love and respect were important to her, and Amber wanted those things desperately. But Amber wasn't Sydney's friend. She wasn't someone to whom Sydney should be confessing this kind of thing.

"Sydney, your father loves you. Very much." Amber tried to keep the mild irritation she felt from her voice. "He only does what he thinks is best for you. If he feels you shouldn't come to Connecticut, then... you won't—"

"B-but," Sydney said, her shoulders rounding, her hands lifting palm up in vehement objection, "I want to see you."

"I know you do." Amber spoke calmly, with a

great deal of assurance. "And I want to see you. If you can't come visit me, then I'll come visit you."

The child looked a little less panicked. But Amber also knew she'd drawn a line. Sydney now knew there were boundaries she couldn't cross with her mother. That Amber had every intention of siding with Jon in parental decisions. And also that Sydney would not be allowed to play one of her parents against the other. Amber supposed there would be many instances like this in the future. She could only hope she'd clearly identify and then follow through in the handling of all of them as adeptly as she had this one.

Sydney tinkered with the paintbrushes that sat on her desk, sulking. But it was evident that she had more she wanted to discuss. Amber remained quiet and waited with patience.

Without looking up, she finally asked, "How come you waited so long to come see me?"

"Come here, hon," Amber coaxed softly. "Come sit next to me and I'll tell you all about it."

And there, in the close confines of the bedroom, Amber did just that. She told her daughter the truth, or rather, specific highlights of the truth. This child needed to know that her mother hadn't abandoned her. That her mother would have moved heaven and earth to have been with her... if she'd only been given the chance.

Soon, the two of them were stretched out on the bed. Sydney asking questions and Amber answering them as best she could.

"But if you didn't know I was alive," Sydney said, "how did you find out about me?"

"I didn't know a thing about you until I saw you at your dad's garage that first day."

"Oh." Sydney reached up and rubbed an itch on her nose. "So that's why you took off so fast."

Amber nodded. "I was... shocked."

"What made you come back to Pine Meadow at all?"

"I, ah..." Amber hesitated, deciding not to bring up the bank account she'd found until she had more information. "I found some paperwork among my father's things that I needed to check on. Paperwork that led me here. So I drove down. And then I met you." It was an awfully simplistic explanation of the facts, and Amber hoped it would suffice.

"So you really did love my dad when you guys were young?"

"Honey, I loved your dad more than words can describe." Amber smiled. "He might not look it now, but he was a rebel. A bad boy. And I fell for him so hard, and so completely, it's scary to me even now."

Sydney giggled. "If you were to talk to my grandmother, she'd say he's still a rebel. But I like that about him. He doesn't let anybody tell him what to do."

"I like that about him, too." The spontaneous comment slipped from Amber's lips.

"Grandmother harps on Dad all the time," Sydney said, sudden sadness tingeing her tone. "About everything. Sometimes I just don't understand her."

Amber only listened. She didn't want to talk about Helen Weston.

Just then a knock on the door had them both twisting to look across the room. Jon stood in the open doorway, and Amber's heart skipped a crazy beat. How long had he been standing there? she wondered. How much of her story had he overheard?

"Hamburgers are on," he said. "If you ladies wouldn't mind, I could use some help carrying the rest of the food out to the picnic table."

"Sure, Dad." Sydney bounded off the bed and out the door like a bouncing ball.

Amber's smile was self-conscious as she stood. "Our daughter sure is energetic."

Jon's chuckle was a sexy rumble deep in his throat.

"Like a nuclear reactor," he said.

She left the room feeling shaky, and knew that it had nothing to do with the heart-to-heart talk she'd just had with Sydney, and everything to do with being in close proximity to the man who had fathered her child.

* * *

In the middle of the following week, Amber was in her hotel room, putting a light coat of mascara on her lashes. She'd become caught in a decadent rut of sleeping late, then going for a long invigorating walk, enjoying a little brunch, and then taking a nice long soak in the tub.

What with college, and then med school, and then completing a difficult residency, Amber had *never* had the luxury of simply being lazy, so she was loving this pampering she was able to give herself now. Her days were pretty much her own and she had no reason to hurry to do anything as her first appointment of each day was meeting her daughter's bus a little after three in the afternoon.

Every day, Amber felt she and Sydney were growing closer, and she loved every single minute they spent together. Of course, spending every afternoon with Sydney meant seeing Jon every day, too. And even though Amber's time with him was minimal, the air sparked and crackled like fireworks on the fourth of July.

The attraction they felt was stronger than ever. And worse, they hadn't had a chance to talk, as they both knew they should. Well, to be completely honest, it wasn't that they hadn't had a chance to talk. It was more they simply hadn't taken the time.

Yes, they were both adults. Yes, they knew they needed to discuss what had happened between them in the woods. Yes, they had to come to some kind of agreement as to how to handle their unruly feelings. But they were also very good at avoiding the issue, she decided as she screwed on the cap of her tube of mascara.

The knock on her hotel room door startled her to the point that she dropped the mascara into the sink. Housekeeping knew her routine by now. The maid knew not to come clean the room until after she'd left at three. Giving the digital clock a quick glance, she saw that it was only two-fifteen.

Jon? Had he finally come to confront her? To force her into talking about—

Again, the silence was interrupted by a knock. Steeling herself, she crossed the small room and opened the door.

Nothing would have prepared her for what awaited on the other side.

"M-M-Mrs. Weston."

The elderly woman's appearance at her door so shocked Amber that her eyes went wide and she felt paralyzed. But immediately following her knee-jerk reaction, she made an attempt to recover, furious at herself for the dim-witted, stuttered greeting.

"Amber," was all the woman said.

Helen Weston's hair was streaked with gray, but was cut and coiffed to perfection. The deep green of her dress was just the right shade to set off her hazel eyes. The black leather handbag she carried matched the pumps on her feet. She looked calm, cool, and utterly professional. But Amber wouldn't have expected Jon's mother to look anything else. Then she noticed something else. The woman also carried a manila file.

Silent seconds ticked by. The woman's chin tipped up. Just a tiny fraction. But the immediate result was that Amber was left feeling looked down upon. Damn!

How was it that Helen Weston, with a single look, could make her feel like a second class citizen?

Doing her best to salvage some self-control, Amber said, "You look like you have something on your mind."

Ignoring Amber's comment, Helen entered the room. And Amber shut the door.

Self-consciousness flared inside her like a beacon when Amber turned and saw the unmade bed, the damp towel that had been tossed over the desk chair.

She snatched up the towel, tossed it into the bathroom and shut the door. "Housekeeping hasn't been in today."

Again, Helen ignored her.

"Sit down," Amber said, offering her the one plush chair in the small room. And she was actually surprised when Jon's mother accepted with a murmured thank-you. Amber turned the desk chair around and sat down.

Then she waited.

During the stiff silence that followed, Amber conjured all manner of things Helen Weston might say to her.

"How dare you come back to Pine Meadow after all this time?"

"I want you packed and gone in twenty-four hours!"

"You stay away from my son and my granddaughter.
"

"Do you really want Sydney to find out what you are? What you came from?"

The possibilities made Amber's insides quiver as she contemplated how she should respond to the anticipated mean questions, angry demands, and sharp accusations.

"So—"

Amber actually started at the woman's first word, but thank goodness Mrs. Weston had her gaze fastened on the purse she clutched tightly in her lap, the folder resting neatly underneath.

"—you came about the account."

It was as though Amber had received a swift kick to her diaphragm. She couldn't breathe, let alone speak.

Silence settled again. Deafening. Claustrophobic.

"Well?"

Helen's hawkish eyes were on Amber now, making her feel like prey.

"The money is the reason you've come back to Pine Meadow?"

There was a strong sense of ownership in her tone when she spoke the name of the town; hoarding and protective, at the same time. Amber heard it and took it to heart.

Mustering her tattered wits, Amber answered, "Yes." She cleared her throat, hoping to strengthen her voice. "That's exactly why I've come."

Helen squared her shoulders and sat up straighter, if that was possible.

"I refused to believe that was you in the bank last week," the woman said. "I just couldn't accept the idea of having to deal with this... distasteful mess all over again."

Just which *distasteful mess* Mrs. Weston was talking about, Amber wasn't certain. Was she referring to her own loathsome behavior where the money was concerned? Or was she talking about Amber and her teen pregnancy?

Amber thought it was a pretty easy guess.

"I'd put the entire matter out of my head," Helen went on. "Hadn't thought about it in years, actually."

"You hadn't thought about it?" Amber wasn't sure which stunned her more, Helen's almost breezy avowal—a declaration, by the way, that made Amber feel completely valueless—or the challenge she heard in her own words. Embers of anger glowed deep in the pit of her belly. "How could you not think about it? How could you not think about me, and my father, and what happened all those years ago, when Sydney is here? Surely you see her. Surely you—"

"Of course, I see her." Helen cut her off smoothly. "I see my granddaughter quite often, in fact. Someone has to see that she's being raised properly." Then she softly added, "Although Jon makes my efforts so difficult." Her head tilted slightly. "But, you see, I don't associate Sydney with..." Her sentence went unfinished as she vaguely waved her hand in a single, short swipe, her face contorting a bit, as if she'd bitten into a thin slice of lemon.

That distasteful mess. Amber almost heard the awful description repeated aloud. And the anger inside her flared. Trying hard to contain her emotions, she decided that it would be in her own best interest to keep her head, not to allow her strong, roiling feelings to rule her tongue. At least, not until after she discovered the information she was looking for about the bank account book she'd found among her father's things.

"*Anyway—*"

Helen smoothed an imagined wrinkle from the immaculate fabric of her dress and Amber got the distinct message that the woman didn't intend to talk about the offensive situation that happened to take place ten years earlier.

"—as I said, I couldn't believe you'd come back to Pine Meadow. I thought my eyes must be playing tricks on me." Mrs. Weston daintily moistened her lipstick-coated lips. "However, I couldn't put the notion aside any longer after this morning."

Amber raised her brows a curious fraction.

"I had a general meeting with the bank staff," she told Amber. "Afterward I was approached by Pete Taylor. He's an employee at the bank. But then you know that, since you talked with him last week. He told me you'd been in to see him."

Folding her hands in her lap, Amber thought it best to simply remain silent for the moment.

"By the way," Helen said, "I'm sorry to hear about your father."

Cold. The woman was cold as a lizard. Sorry was the last thing she was feeling. That was clear.

Amber realized that Helen Weston only offered the condolence because that's what propriety dictated. There was certainly no sympathy or comfort in the offer.

Amber couldn't help but feel sorry for Jon that he'd had to grow up with such a woman as his mother.

"If you'll fill out the paperwork that Pete provided you with," Helen said, rushing into the business at hand, "I can see that the account is turned over to you today. And you can be on your way back to... wherever it is you've been these past ten years."

As she spoke, she picked up and opened the file she brought with her. She got up and handed Amber some forms.

Listed on the crisp white paper was a printout of her father's account; the date of the initial deposit, as well as the dates and amounts of the accruing interest. Amber stared down at the sheets. Finally she rubbed the fingers of her free hand back and forth across her forehead. Then she gazed up at Mrs. Weston and shook her head.

"You do want the money, don't you?" she asked Amber. "It was your father's. Now it's yours."

For a moment, Amber didn't trust herself to

speak. What did this woman think? That she could stuff some money into Amber's hand, pat her on the head, and scoot her out of town? Helen Weston's audacity infuriated her.

Calm down. The silent advice made Amber pause. *Hold back that anger for a few minutes more.*

She fortified herself with a deep inhalation, and quietly asked, "Where did the money come from, Mrs. Weston?' '

The woman's gaze went flat. "How am I supposed to know that? It was your father's life savings, maybe?" She shrugged. "It isn't my business to ask where my customers get their money. It's only my business to carefully protect that money. And that's exactly what I've done. Now what I'd suggest you do is—"

"Just stop it!" Amber barely suppressed the overwhelming urge to fling the papers right in Helen's face. But instead, she crushed them in one fist as she jumped from the chair and paced the length of the small hotel room. "You know this money came from you. You and your husband. You deposited this money in my father's name to ease your conscience."

Helen's lips pursed. "I guess I should have expected you to say something so... ugly."

"It's the truth," Amber spit out. "And I do agree. It's ugly as hell." She gritted her teeth. "But you want to know what's even uglier?"

She watched Helen grow utterly still, her eyes narrowing warily.

Her tone was low and ruthless as she said, "What that money bought."

"Don't," Helen said, her voice a raspy whisper. But Amber barreled ahead, the flames of her anger burning bright. "That money bought a child. My child," she said, viciously jabbing at her chest with her index finger. "That money bought my happiness. That money bought all the years I missed with my daughter. I didn't get to see her take her first step. Speak her first word. I didn't get to hear her recite the alphabet. Or get on the school bus for the first time. I missed it all! I missed everything."

She swiped at a lock of hair that had fallen into her face. "Everything," she continued, "except the grief." Amber felt tears well in her eyes. "I spent years grieving for a baby that I was told was born dead. And all I have to show for that is a lump sum of cash that's sitting in Weston Savings and Loan." The harsh bark of laughter erupted painfully around the huge knot of sorrow in her throat.

"Granted, it is a lot of money. Boy, this cost you plenty, didn't it? I remember the doctor that delivered my baby. You must have paid him a great deal to lie like he did. And the nurse. She, too, must have cost you. How much did you pay them, Helen?"

Her use of the woman's first name was meant to reveal the tremendous disrespect Amber felt for Jon's mother at this moment, and blinding fury was the motivating factor. That, combined with the huge sense of being wronged.

Helen Weston's chest rose and fell, rapidly, the only sign that she was feeling any emotion at all.

"I paid them a lot." She kept perfect control of herself. "A whole lot."

Their gazes locked tight.

"So," Amber said, "you admit it. You admit to *buying* my child. *Robbing* me of raising my own baby." The older woman winced. What? Amber wondered. Was she actually causing fissures in that facade of granite Helen was wearing?

"I only did what I thought was best for my boy," she said.

"He was a man," Amber said pointedly. "A twenty-year-old man."

"He was a *child*. A naive boy who knew nothing.

Nothing, about life. Nothing about goals. And he was about to throw away everything."

A thin sheen of perspiration glistened on Helen's upper lip. "But then," she added as a quiet aside, "he's always been bent on throwing away everything."

The woman's complicated statement held hidden messages that evidently dealt with the present, but Amber was too involved with what happened in the past to give it much notice.

"If you think Jon becoming a father meant he was ruining his life," Amber said, "then why didn't you just leave me and my baby alone? Why didn't you just let me raise my daughter?"

"You? Raise a Weston?"

Amber wasn't hurt by Helen's insults; she was simply amazed that the woman tossed them out in such a natural, matter-of-fact manner.

"You had nothing," Helen continued. "You had no prospects of ever having anything. No breeding, no background, no education."

Pride surged up within her. "Well, I have an education now. In fact, I'm practicing medicine. I'm a full-fledged medical doctor."

Her attempt to impress Jon's mother fell flat as it became apparent that the declaration didn't affect the woman in the least. And the effort left Amber feeling hollow and more than a little irritated with herself for having tried.

Helen's only response was, "Ten years ago, you had nothing."

Tucking her bottom lip firmly between her teeth, Amber remained silent. She couldn't argue with the truth.

"Amber," Helen began. Then she paused, inhaled deeply and squared her shoulders. "I don't expect you to understand the reasons behind what my husband and I did all those years ago."

Her voice barely a whisper, Amber said, "Don't forget to include my father on your list of culprits."

"Your father..." Helen Weston shook her head. "Your father did exactly what we told him to do. We talked him into believing that sending Sydney to us was the right thing to do. For you. For Jon. For everyone concerned. And he believed us because we were right."

She unlatched her purse and pulled out a tissue. "You and your father couldn't offer Sydney anything. While my husband and I... we had everything to offer the child."

Amber's spine straightened as a thought struck

her with force. "You planned to raise Sydney yourself."

"I did. I planned to bring her up as a proper young lady." Helen went quiet, then she added, "But you know what they say about the best laid plans."

Humorless irony tugged at one corner of Amber's mouth. "I guess that means Jon had other plans."

"Didn't he always?" Daintily Helen dabbed her chin with the tissue. "We hadn't had that child under our roof for eighteen months before Jon up and proclaimed he couldn't work in the bank. He reneged on his promise to join the family business. That boy's stubbornness killed his father. And then he moved out of Weston House. He took that child off to a tiny little apartment. Even after all I tried to do for him. Even after all the money I doled out. He still managed to ruin his life. His life *and* Sydney's."

Confusion knit Amber's brow. "But I don't see how he's ruined his life. He's doing what he wants. His auto shop seems successful enough."

"Please." Helen sniffed. "Jon struggles from month to month."

"He has money problems?"

"He hasn't come to me for money yet," Helen said. "But he will, you mark my words. And he isn't able to give Sydney the things she needs."

Amber thought about her cheerful, contented daughter, remembering her easy laughter, her quick wit. "Sydney seems happy enough to me. I think Jon's doing a great job—"

"That child is a mess," Helen interrupted. "She's always got some tool or other in her hands. And she's always covered from head to toe in axle grease. It's horrible."

Remembering how Sydney's eyes lit up when she told Amber about the car she built with her father, Amber decided her daughter was a normal, boisterous ten-year-old, grease or no grease. Sydney and Jon were doing what they loved to do. And they were having fun and spending lots of time together doing it, too. Time that would bond their father/daughter relationship forever. Their lives seemed healthy. And very happy. But arguing that point with Helen Weston would be futile.

After a moment, Helen said, "I never in my life thought I'd find myself in this position."

A frown planted itself in Amber's forehead. She couldn't fathom what the woman meant.

"I never imagined," she continued, "that I'd have to ask for your discretion."

"My...?" Amber shook her head, having no clue where the conversation was going.

"Amber, Jon and I don't have the best of relationships." Helen paused long enough to pat the tissue against her upper lip. "We didn't ten years ago, and we still don't today. But I love my son. Just like any mother loves her child. And I don't know what it would do to our relationship if he were ever to find out about... the money I paid your father."

Her breath left her in a whoosh. "Jon doesn't know." Feelings flooded through her, a powerful mixture of relief and elation. He hadn't been aware of the conspiracy to steal her child from her. The revelation was overwhelming. And for a long moment she let herself bask in it.

Suddenly, she was aware that Helen had grown still and quiet, pensive as she waited for Amber to offer some reaction.

"You're asking me to keep the bank account a secret," Amber said. "You don't want me to tell Jon."

"That's exactly what I'm asking."

Amber thought a moment, then asked, "Why?

Why would you think I'd do something like that for you? After what you did to me."

"You won't be doing it for me," Helen said softly. "You'll be doing it for Jon."

That took the wind out of Amber's sails.

"You used to have deep feelings for my son..."

A shiver raced up Amber's spine as she pondered those potent feelings, and how they had returned, full-force, since she'd come back to Pine Meadow.

"I'm asking you to think about him," she went on. "Think about what's best for Jon. He'd be hurt if he knew. Our relationship is tenuous at best. If he found out about this, it would destroy what little we do have."

Amber looked at this woman, thoughts ricocheting in her brain like so many ping-pong balls. Helen was pushing Amber into silence. Silence that would save Jon from being hurt. Silence that would save Helen from being hurt. Well...

"What about me?" she blurted. "What about the pain I felt when I was told my baby died? What about the grief I suffered? The long years of grief?"

Helen sighed. "I can't do anything about that.

Amber, I can't give you an apology for something I'm not sorry about."

Lowering her gaze, Amber noticed that Helen had begun to twist the tissue in her fingers.

"I am sorry your father didn't transfer the money to another bank," she continued. "I am sorry he didn't spend it. That he didn't burn the bankbook along with all the statements. But I can't apologize for doing what I thought was best for everyone concerned. For you and Jon. And especially for Sydney."

Chapter Nine

In the end, Amber agreed to keep silent about the money Jon's parents deposited in the account to her father as payment for Sydney. Amber wanted badly to believe she hadn't agreed to be a party in this plot—and plot was exactly how she thought of it, a plot to keep Jon in the dark—for Helen Weston.

Jon's mother was a cold and calculating woman. She was someone Amber had, for as long as she could remember, feared. Someone who had made her feel unworthy.

Amber had thought that when she'd returned to Pine Meadow, all grown up with doctorate in hand and success in her future, that she'd no longer feel inferior. She'd been wrong. Helen Weston would never look at Amber as an equal. Never.

What amazed Amber the most was that Jon's mother had been the one who had acted in such a despicable manner, yet the woman could still look down her nose at others.

So why had Amber agreed to keep the money a secret from Jon?

There were several reasons. Sydney had been her number one motivation. Amber didn't even want to begin to imagine how devastating it would be for her daughter to find out what Helen had done. How the child's own grandmother had completely severed any chance Sydney had of being raised by her own mother.

Then there was Jon. Helen had tweaked something inside Amber when she'd played on Amber's past feelings for Jon. There had been a time when Amber had loved the man with all of her heart, with every nuance of her soul. He, too, would be devastated to discover his mother's wicked deception. In honor of what they had once shared—not to mention the overwhelming emotions he stirred in her since her return to town—Amber thought it best to keep the news from him.

And then there had been the part Amber's father had played in the whole horrible scheme.

Yes, Amber continued to feel utterly disappointed in her dad for allowing himself to be caught up in the manipulative plot. But he'd given her all he could over the years— even though he'd taken away so very much. Amber sighed sadly when she thought of all he'd denied her. However, she still loved him. How could she not? He was her father. He was family. He'd taken care of her. Loved her. Sacrificed for her. Out of respect for his memory, Amber decided to keep his one indiscretion a secret.

"Happy Birthday!"

Sydney's friends began to sing the Birthday Song as the waitress of the pizza parlor brought to the table the cake with its ten flaming candles. Amber gazed at her grinning daughter and joined in the singing.

A heated, poignant rush washed over her—emotion Amber had discovered was pure maternal love. There was nothing like it, nothing to compare to the intense feelings a mother felt toward her child. She was blessed to be here at Sydney's tenth birthday party. Blessed to know her daughter. Truly blessed to have the chance to hug her, love her, the chance to mold and guide the young woman Sydney would become.

Amber realized suddenly that if she hadn't come across that tainted bank account, she might never have discovered she even had a daughter. The idea left her feeling a twinge of bleakness at the prospect, then all the more content that circumstances had turned out as they had.

Once the last notes of the song faded, Jon called out, "Don't forget to make a wish before you blow out those candles, Syd."

A smile glittered in his vivid green gaze, and Amber's heart *ka-chunked* in her chest. Almost a week had passed since she'd conspired with Helen, and every single time she was with Jon she was bothered by the acute awareness that she was lying to him.

Yes, she knew that keeping the secret was saving him from being hurt, but she still felt guilt-ridden. And that guilt was compounded mightily by the allure they battled daily.

She wanted him so badly she could almost taste the sweet desire that pulsed through her veins. He wanted her, too. That was clear to her every moment they were together. The longing in the looks he gave her couldn't be hidden, even if he'd tried, which he didn't. And there were times Amber was certain that, if Sydney were to leave them alone for even a single second, he'd reach out for her, touch her in a way that would make her writhe with pleasure. But, luckily, they hadn't had the occasion to be alone.

Amber sighed. Luck had very little to do with it. She'd made sure they hadn't had a chance to be by themselves. Because she was frightened witless of being alone with him now that she knew he was completely innocent of wrongdoing. She was so confused by her feelings. By the intensity of the emotions that grew, day by day.

Knowing he was blameless should have freed her, should have erased every bit of the doubt she felt about acting on her physical attraction, her overwhelming need.

But the thing holding her at bay was the guilt. Keeping Helen's secret felt wrong, and guilt constantly poked and prodded at her conscience.

As Sydney busied herself opening brightly colored packages, her friends chattering in delight, Amber felt Jon's eyes drawing her attention. Sure enough, he was staring at her. In a manner that made his sensuous thoughts quite clear. His expression made her feel as if they were the only two people alive on earth. Her cheeks, neck, and chest heated. Slowly he got up from the table and came to stand beside her, never once taking his eyes off her face.

"I need you." His whisper was for her ears alone.

Her eyes widened, a delicious shiver shimmying across her skin.

He quickly added, "I need to talk to you."

For a brief instant, Amber wondered if he was amending his statement, but one look at his handsome face and she was certain she hadn't misheard his original words—or his intent. The need clouding his gaze was absolute proof that her ears hadn't failed her.

"I can't stand this any longer," he told her.

The desire simmering in his voice made her pulse go haywire, her blood pressure skyrocket.

"We have to talk."

She understood. She, too, had suffered the profound tension that throbbed and pulsed, seeming to have a life of its own.

Reaching up, she crossed her arms, smoothed her hands up and down her biceps and acquiesced with a small nod.

"You'll follow me back to my house?" he asked softly.

Again she nodded.

"Sydney's asked to go to Wendy's sleepover," he said. "We'll have the house to ourselves."

That news scared Amber half to death. And excited her beyond belief.

He turned back to the party taking place in the pizza parlor, a "friends only" affair that Sydney had requested. Syd had told Amber that she didn't relish the "family" party she'd have to endure later this week. A stuffy party with no kids her own age, only aunts and uncles... and her grandmother.

Amber was happy that Jon had agreed to such a gathering as this one with its gooey pizza, sodas, ice cream, and cake, and a horde of squealing, gabbling girlfriends. Oh, and presents. Lots of presents. Amber was also pleased to be a part of Sydney's special day, the first birthday she'd ever celebrated with her daughter. But Amber really disliked the fact that her merriment was hampered by anxiety over her impending "talk" with Jon.

* * *

The moon hung fat in the sky, so close to the earth that Amber could easily see the craters with their gray-blue valleys against the stark whiteness of the orb. The night was lit up so bright that few stars could be seen twinkling in the silky black expanse.

As she'd promised, Amber had followed Jon back to his house. Sydney had gathered together her pajamas, slippers, and toothbrush, and then Jon and Amber had taken their daughter to Wendy's house. April and Wendy bounded out the front door and the girls had giggled themselves silly right there in the front yard. The one thing Amber would never forget, however, was that, before she and Jon could drive off, Sydney had rushed back to the car at the last moment and planted a sweet kiss on Amber's cheek.

"Bye," Sydney had whispered. "I will see ya tomorrow."

The question in her daughter's soft brown eyes practically split Amber's heart in two. "Of course, you will," she'd assured Sydney softly. Sydney had then gone around to the driver's side of the car and had given her dad a good-night kiss.

The ride back to Jon's had been made in silence. And Amber was relieved to have a few minutes to ponder again this wondrous thing called motherhood. The heart-wrenching emotions Amber experienced when she was with Sydney were all so new to her. Overwhelming in their proportions, she sometimes thought her heart simply could not hold everything she felt for the beautiful child she had given birth to. Amber wondered if the magnitude of her feelings might wear off or wind down. Would the poignancy, the deep richness of the emotions she felt wane with the passing of time? Was the overpowering nature of her feelings due to the fact that she'd missed the first ten years of her daughter's life?

As soon as they had arrived at Jon's home, he'd ushered her out back and then he went inside to heat up some cider. When he returned and handed her a steaming mug, she was still contemplating the disturbing idea.

"When Sydney kissed me," she said quietly, settling the bottom of the mug against one palm, "my heart filled with so much love, I thought it would burst like a balloon." Jon eased himself down beside her on the wooden bench, one corner of his mouth hitching up.

"I wonder..." She paused, a sudden sense of shyness creeping up on her. "I wonder if women who have been with their children from the very beginning continue to feel this awesome, breathtaking—" she shook her head as words escaped her "—emotion?" His mouth pulled into a full-fledged smile.

"I can't speak for moms," he told her. "But as Sydney's dad, I can say that every time she hugs me, or kisses my cheek, or even when she graces me with a simple smile, she just takes away my breath. She always has." His tone lowered as he added, "I expect she always will."

Amber swallowed a sip of the cider, the taste of apple and cinnamon both sweet and tangy on her tongue. She lowered the mug, and studied Jon's handsome face. He was such a good and loving father. A pure-hearted and decent person. And in that moment—that very instant—she was struck with a stupefying revelation.

She loved this man. She had never stopped loving him in all the years they had spent apart.

What she had taken for mere physical attraction was a thin veil that disguised the deep and powerful love that churned within her, that had lain dormant for so very long.

There were reasons why she shouldn't. Plenty of reasons.

He'd hurt her all those years ago. With his rejection. With his angry accusations and name-calling. He'd caused her pain and sorrow, humiliation and anguish. So much pain, she'd feared at times, she simply wouldn't survive it.

But she had.

Now here she sat, ten years later, facing the man in whom she had placed all her hopes, all her dreams. The man she had loved—*still loved*—with every fiber of her being.

And he sat beside her, looking at her with unmistakable, unadulterated desire shining in his green eyes.

Jon leaned over and took the mug from her hands. Then he set them both on the ground. When he straightened, he slid closer to her until their knees and thighs were pressed together, and the heat of his body seeped into her skin.

"I love Sydney," he said. "And your coming to Pine Meadow has been good for her. I'm happy about that. I'm happy that you've become important to her. A necessary part of her life. I'd been worried that she wasn't getting the feminine influence she needed. Now, I know you're going to take care of that. Your being a part of our daughter's life only means good things for Sydney. Even though, I realize, there are still plenty of things you and I need to work out. But..."

His face pinched, as if he was feeling a discomfiting emotion.

"But I don't want to talk about Sydney tonight," he admitted softly. "I want to talk about us. You. And me. And this... this *thing* that's practically eating us alive."

An undeniable intensity emanated off him, but she was also vaguely aware that he'd slid his hand across the back of the seat, that he'd inadvertently begun to toy with a small lock of her hair, almost as if he couldn't keep his hands to himself.

She knew exactly how he felt. She ached to touch him, to run her hands over his chest, to at least take his hand in hers, entwine her fingers with his. But not knowing whether he felt good or bad about this potent magnetism between them, she held the urges at bay. He might want her, but he might not want to want her. Before she acted on her own impulses, she had to know how he felt about his.

He smoothed his index finger along the outer curve of her ear, slowly, sensually. And his gaze darkened.

"I want so badly to kiss you," he said. "To hold you against me. But I just can't. I can't allow myself the pleasure."

A heavy sigh escaped him. A sigh that conveyed all the effort it was taking to keep himself from giving in to temptation—the temptation of *her*. A tiny thrill shot through her.

"Not until we talk." His gaze roamed over her face, lingering on her mouth. "Not until I tell you what's on my mind. Not until I—" he looked her in the eyes "—apologize."

"Jon..."

He touched his fingertips gently against her lips. "Shh," he crooned. "Let me finish. This has bothered me for—" his exhalation was rueful "—*ever*. Ever since I said those horrible things to you all those years ago."

His fingertips trailed from her mouth to her jaw. "A simple 'I'm sorry,'" he continued, "just isn't enough. I need to explain. To try to make you understand what I was going through back then."

Amber didn't want to remember those awful moments, but in an instant, she was back there. In that frightful place. That frightful time. At the vulnerable age of seventeen.

The angry look on Jon's face had been enough to bring her to tears. But the hostile words he'd flung at her had been like deadly arrows he'd aimed straight at her heart, and he couldn't have been more successful in killing her spirit had he wielded an actual weapon.

"How could you have let this happen?" he'd shouted at her just after she'd tearfully revealed her pregnancy to him.

Amber didn't remember the exact sequence of his mean and furious accusations. All she remembered was the pain she felt as he pelted her with each one.

"You're trying to trap me. You don't want me to succeed. You're not interested in making anything of yourself. You'd be happy to be stuck for the rest of your life in a dingy little one-room apartment. With half a dozen hungry mouths to feed. My parents were right about you."

He had spit out other slurs against her. Insulting and slanderous. Hurtful beyond belief. But the one that wounded her the most, the one she would never forget, was when he'd agreed with his parents' opinion of her.

The Westons—Jon included—would always think of her as second-rate.

Amber had stood there silently and had taken everything Jon had doled out. She'd absorbed his anger.

Submitted to his wrath. Because she had felt she

deserved it. She'd felt to blame. She'd gotten pregnant. In her innocent mind, she decided he was justified in dealing her any punishment he saw fit. And punish her, he had. With irrefutable rejection.

"I don't want to have anything more to do with you."

His parting words rang in her head, like the reverberating ring of a death knell even all these years later. She blinked, a single, silent tear slipping down her face, its momentum tickling her skin, bringing her out of the nightmare of the past and back into the present.

"Ah, Amber." Jon's voice was raw, and he gently swiped at the moist track on the side of her nose with the pad of his thumb. "The things I said still hurt you. Even now."

His observation didn't require a reply. She couldn't very well deny her pain, the pain she knew was evident on her face, in her tears. But there was something she needed to say, something she'd wanted to say way back then but was never given the chance.

"I'm sorry I ruined everything for us," she whispered; her voice sounded bruised and bleak. "I didn't mean to get pregnant—"

"*We* got pregnant, Amber," he interrupted. "That was something that happened when we were together." He shook his head. "And if anything, I'm the one who should shoulder most of the blame. I was the older one. I never should have enticed you to become... physically intimate. You were just a kid, really." He gazed off. "The first time we had sex you were only sixteen." Again, he shook his head with regret. "The only excuse I have is that I was young. Immature. Hormones had me listening to the wrong part of my anatomy. And, Amber, like stupid kids everywhere, I thought I was invincible. I thought we were. I never thought in a million years something like that would happen to us."

His intense gaze commanded her complete attention. "I had no right to blame you," he said softly. "But it was so damned easy. Easier than blaming myself. Which is what I *should* have done. I should have taken responsibility for my actions." His hand went slack on her shoulder for a moment, his voice dropping to a mere whisper as he added, "Our lives would have turned out so differently if I had."

Every instinct in her told her to be accepting and forgiving. But the years of agony she'd suffered through, the grief that had totally snuffed out her joy, the blame she'd shouldered all these years, cried out for retribution... or at least some kind of acknowledgment.

"So," she found herself saying, "why didn't you?" He whispered her name on a groan. She heard his deep remorse, and for a moment she was sorry she'd confronted him when he was already trying to apologize. However, even though she regretted her question, she didn't recant it. She'd suffered enough to deserve an answer.

"My life had been a wreck, a total disaster for about a month prior to..."

Jon looked heavenward, evidently searching for a word or phrase to describe the event that initiated their terrible breakup.

"Your announcement," he said.

Amber remembered how he'd changed, remembered how hurt and confused she'd been by the distance he slowly but surely placed between them.

"You see," he continued, "my parents had found out about us. They started this campaign against you. Against our relationship. It was clear they wanted me to stop seeing you. They also began to actively lobby for change in other areas of my life. They threatened me, harassed me, pressured me, every day. Then they began lecturing me about my future. They told me it was time for me to get serious about my life. It was time to put away the toys, and by that they meant my motorcycle, my jeans, my leather jacket, my love of cars. They urged me, again and again, to find some respect for myself. To dress up in a business suit. To go work in the bank. They made this ready-made career they had in mind for me sound so... right."

For the life of her, Amber couldn't understand what was so new about that. The way she remembered it, from the very first time she and Jon had talked, he'd complained about his parents' disapproval of his behavior. He'd always felt resentful that they couldn't accept him and love him for who he was. And he'd hated the idea of their trying to make him into something he wasn't.

"But," she said, "none of that was really unusual, was it? It's what they'd always done."

He nodded. "But something changed after they discovered our relationship. The lectures became more intense. They focused on the fact that you were so young. Too young to be influenced by me." He sighed. "And then there was the change in my dad. He started taking time to be with me. To show an interest in what I thought about things. I'd always believed my dad couldn't stand the sight of me. To have his attention... well, it was something I'd never had before. And every time Dad and I were together, my mother was so... happy."

Jon studied her a moment.

"They were my parents, Amber. I wanted them to be proud of me. I wanted to make them happy. Is that so wrong?"

She couldn't help but wonder just how many parents, her own father included, played on their children's desire to be loved and accepted to get them to toe the line. The thought saddened her, and she decided then and there that she would never force her own daughter to do or be anything other than what Sydney wanted for herself.

"For the first time in my life," Jon said, "I seemed to have my parents' approval. And to keep it, I ended up promising to go to work in the bank." He paused a moment. "I had no idea how I was going to tell you. I was so afraid I would lose your respect. I was still trying to find a way to explain, when you told me you were going to have a baby."

He ran his fingers through his dark hair. "The news was earth-shattering, to say the least. How was I ever going to explain to my father that I screwed up? Again."

Amber noticed he no longer touched her. That he'd even backed away from her an inch or so, and she got the distinct impression that he felt he didn't deserve to be near her, to touch her, when he was revealing his motive behind rejecting her. And from the anguish displayed on his handsome face, she suspected the worst was yet to come.

"I couldn't disappoint my dad," Jon said. "I just couldn't. So in a moment of weakness... a moment of pure panic, I turned on you. Completely. I blamed you for everything. It was so much easier to do that than to go home and face losing my father's respect altogether."

Tilting her head to one side, Amber simply looked at him. She understood. She really did. She would have done anything to make her own father happy. He'd been all she had. And even though she now knew her father had taken part in keeping her from Sydney all these years, Amber realized that didn't change the fact that she loved him. So she understood why Jon had done what he had done, said what he had said. She was actually a little relieved because all this time she had believed his mean and spiteful words had been caused by something else. She'd thought all those years ago that Jon had suspected she was pregnant even before she'd discovered the fact herself. That he'd become standoffish because he couldn't cope with the idea of becoming a father. She'd thought he'd rejected her because he didn't want her. Didn't want their child. To find out he'd turned away from her because of his parents actually softened the blow of what had happened to them.

One corner of his mouth curled in a sad smile. "How does that old saying go? The one that says, 'You always hurt the one you love, the one you shouldn't hurt at all.' Well, that's how I've always felt about the way we parted. I hurt you. And I never should have. I'm terribly sorry. And I hope you'll forgive me."

Amber reached out and took his hand in hers. "You're forgiven."

The smile he gave her made her feel warm and wonderful. She was glad to know the truth, to have the shadows of the past cleared up, and he seemed relieved to have had the chance to explain.

He rubbed his thumb over the hills and valleys of her knuckles. "It's so funny how fate works. As it turned out I ended up disappointing my parents anyway. I couldn't continue working at the bank...

even though I tried. Hard. Especially after Sydney came to us. Mom and Dad promised to help me raise Sydney as long as I proceeded along on the right path. The path they chose for me. But I just couldn't. I hated being cooped up in that stuffy office, working with numbers all day. It just wasn't me." One of his shoulders hitched up a fraction. "So I quit."

Amber remained silent, feeling it best to simply listen.

"Dad died shortly thereafter," he went on. "The doctor said it was a brain aneurysm, but my mother was sure he'd died because he was so worried, so upset. About me. About my future. And Syd's."

Jon's stubbornness killed his father. Amber remembered Helen Weston's words. At the time Amber had thought it had simply been a figure of speech, a way for Jon's mother to convey the depth of her husband's turmoil. However, now Amber was left wondering if Helen Weston really did believe what she'd said. If that was so, Amber thought it was a horrible burden Helen had placed on her son. An awful thought she'd put in Jon's head.

"I took Sydney away from Weston House," Jon

told her. "I needed to make a life for us. A life we could be happy with."

Amber eagerly pointed out, "It seems as though you've succeeded at that. Sydney is happy. She's well-adjusted. She's intelligent. She's an all-around great kid. You've done a terrific job."

His embarrassed grin charmed her to the tips of her toes.

After a moment he said, "You know, when everything's said and done, we do have to admit that some good came out of your, ah, going away."

Curiosity had her brows raising a fraction.

"If you'd have stayed here," he explained, "you'd never have had the opportunity to go to college. You'd never have become a doctor."

With no hesitation, Amber replied, "I'd give it all up in a heartbeat... to have been able to be here to raise Sydney."

He slid his hand up to tenderly cup her cheek as he silently studied her gaze.

"But you have so much more to offer Sydney now," he said, "because of the hand fate dealt us."

Amber pressed her palm to the back of his hand. "It's important to me that you know our child means everything to me. That I want to be there for her. That I want only what's best for her."

He whispered, "I want to believe you."

And then he covered her mouth with his.

His kiss short-circuited her thinking. All she did was *feel*. Warm, silky, sensuous sensations. His touch, his kiss, had always had the ability to leave her breathless, thoughtless, senseless. And this time was no exception.

Threading her fingers into his thick hair, she pulled him even closer. The scent of him, the taste of him, the feel of his hard body so close to hers, was enough to make her nearly wild with need.

His breath was erratic in her ear, his desire clearly evident in his ardent kiss, and that only served to heat the passion in her blood even more.

"I want us to try again, Amber."

His words were an urgent whisper against her hot, moist mouth.

"I want us to have the chance that was taken away from us ten years ago."

Tiny bursts of joy exploded inside her, like dozens of miniature fireworks, colorful and glittering. The idea of spending the rest of her life with this man was overwhelming, to say the least. But a dark cloud hovered over the celebration going on in her head.

I want to believe you, his words echoed in her brain.

He hadn't said he believed her when she'd told him what Sydney meant to her. He'd said he *wanted to.* There was a nuance of difference—a nuance that had a significant effect on her.

Doubt was inferred in his statement. About what? she couldn't help but wonder. Doubt about her feelings for Sydney? Doubt about her future intentions? Amber didn't think so. She was sure the uncertainty he was obviously feeling hinged on the past. On her behavior in the past.

He's still holding on to the notion that I sent Sydney back to him, she silently realized. He still believes I lied to him about the circumstances surrounding Sydney's birth.

She wanted so badly to tell him her story again. To explain that she was innocent of any wrongdoing. That she was the one who had been wronged. By her own father. And by Jon's parents.

However, it was with a sinking heart that she realized that the one piece to the puzzle that would exonerate her, prove her innocence beyond all doubt, was the secret she'd promised to keep from him.

Her whole body trembled. And although the tiny kisses he planted on her neck and jaw were utterly tantalizing, she knew the quaking inside her was caused by the helplessness she suddenly felt over this predicament.

"Wait," she murmured.

Amber didn't want him to have any doubts about her.

"Jon, stop."

He kissed her mouth again, and then lifted his head just enough to look into her face. What could she say? her frantic mind wondered. How could she clear his doubts if she couldn't tell him the full truth?

She studied his gaze, vying for time.

"We need to slow down." The words slipped past her lips. "We can't rush this."

The chuckle vibrating in his chest was deep and sexy. "Oh," he said, "but I want to rush it. We've wasted too much time already."

"Lots of time *has* passed." She latched onto the excuse with both hands. "That's my point exactly. You've been through so much. And so have I. We don't know each other as well as we once did. We need to take our time. We need to..."

She let the sentence fade, feeling as though her bumbling discourse sounded much too lame for belief. Surely he'd see her plea for what it truly was... pure evasion.

The kiss he placed on one corner of her mouth was so gentle, so sweet, her heart constricted with heavy guilt.

His green eyes were clear and shining with generosity as he said, "I'm happy to give us all the time you think we need."

Chapter Ten

She had to tell him. There was no way around it.

How could she keep this secret from Jon and expect them to share any kind of long-term, loving relationship? It would be impossible. Totally inconceivable.

Amber paced from one end of Jon's kitchen to the other. She'd met Sydney at the bus, fixed her a snack, and then shooed her daughter to her room to study for tomorrow's spelling test.

During the three days that had passed since Sydney's birthday, Amber had stiffened each and every time Jon had reached for her. She wanted so badly to feel his hands on her, but the guilty secret she harbored hovered continuously on the edges of her brain.

When she was alone in her hotel room, she'd

allowed herself to dream of being with him. Of the happy family life she, Jon, and Sydney could have together. A ready-made family. She'd even gone so far as to plan exactly how to go about leaving the family medical practice in Connecticut and opening her own office here in Pine Meadow. There was certainly no reason why she couldn't. Her doctorate made her eligible to practice medicine anywhere. Of course, she'd have to look into procuring a state license...

But a heavy dark feeling in the pit of her gut burst the bubble of every happy dream she conjured, the gloom caused by the knowledge that she was concealing from Jon the full truth. The fact that she was saving him from being hurt didn't ease her guilt one iota. The secret she kept was like a towering mountain between her and Jon. Between her and true happiness.

She simply had to tell him.

After she did, after they climbed the dangerous, and most probably hurtful, cliffs representing the whole truth regarding the past, then and only then would they be free to plan their future together.

And, oh, what a future it would be.

Jon pushed open the kitchen door, and Amber stopped dead in her tracks. His expression was grim, his stance tight with stress. The aura he presented, the mood fairly vibrating from him, was tense, pent-up, disapproving.

Amber's first thought was that he'd argued with one of his mechanics, or a customer. However, that thought flitted away when she saw the glare he focused directly on her.

"What is it?" she asked. "What's wrong?"

"You didn't come back to Pine Meadow because of Sydney."

His tone was low, ominous, and trepidation clenched in Amber's stomach as though it were a huge fist.

She frowned. "Of course, I didn't," she said. "I told you from the very beginning that I didn't know about Sydney until I saw her for the first time in your shop."

"That's your story and you're sticking to it, huh?"

Amber's brow knitted tighter and she nodded. Then she asked, "Is there some reason why I shouldn't?"

"You could say that."

It was when he lifted his arm a few inches that she noticed for the first time the papers he held in his hand.

"You want to try to explain this?" He tossed the loose pages onto the tile-topped island standing between them.

Amber reached out, not picking them up, but only turning them around to face her. Her eyes widened. There in front of her was her father's bank account information. Only her father's name wasn't listed on the account—*hers* was.

Jon's mother must have gone into the computer at the bank and changed the name of the account holder... without Amber's permission. There had to be some sort of law against such an action.

"Why didn't you tell me you'd spoken with my mother?" he asked, accusation weighing heavy in his query.

Still reeling under the idea that Helen Weston could have done such a thing, Amber automatically answered, "Because I didn't want you to be hurt. I didn't want Sydney to be hurt."

Or my father's memory to be defiled, the silent words died on her tongue. Amber doubted Jon would be the least interested in her last reason for withholding information from him.

"At least you're owning up to knowing about the account," he said. "When Mom came to see me, she'd told me to expect you to deny any wrongdoing."

Ten years ago, the only wrongdoing Amber could have been accused of would have been that of giving herself, body, and soul, to the boy she'd loved. But here and now, she was guilty of having connived with that untrustworthy woman. For that, Amber felt plain awful, especially when that unholy alliance—one she'd agreed to for what she'd thought were such noble reasons—was being used against her.

"I heard you tell Sydney you'd come back to town because of some 'business papers' you'd found," Jon continued. "I never would have imagined Weston Savings and Loan business was what you meant." He glared. "You came back for the money. Period."

The allegation he charged her with was like the final slam of a judge's gavel. Verdict rendered. No further evidence allowed. No further arguments accepted.

She tipped up her chin, refusing to let him see how his words hurt her.

"I did not come back *for* the money," she said quietly. "I came back *about* the money."

"Don't waste my time with semantics!"

His shout actually made her jump.

"There's no need to raise your voice," she said. "Sydney will hear you."

They both grew quiet and still when they heard Sydney's rushed footfalls on the bare wood.

"Dad?" Sydney didn't come into the room, evidently feeling the angry tension pulsing in the air. Hovering in the doorway, she asked, "Is everything okay?"

"Go back to your room, Sydney." Jon didn't take his hard gaze off Amber as he addressed his daughter behind him. "I need to talk to your mother. Alone."

"But…" The child's voice faded.

The frown of confusion Amber saw on Sydney's brow just about broke her heart.

"Mom, what's going on?"

"Honey, your dad and I need to talk," Amber said gently. "Listen to your dad. Go back to your room. I'll come back and say good-night before I leave. I promise."

"But I heard Dad yell."

"Sydney." There was a clear warning in Jon's voice. "Go."

The child hung her head and turned on her heel. Amber's heart ached to reassure Sydney. To tell her that everything would be okay. But she couldn't. Because she didn't know if everything *would* be okay.

Jon glanced at the empty hallway, then called out, "Shut your door," and immediately, the click of Sydney's bedroom door latch sounded.

When he turned his eyes on Amber, she likened them to chips of cold stone.

"What I can't fathom," he said, "is why all the romantic games?"

His tone clearly conveyed that he was gaining momentum, that he didn't want her to answer, that he wanted to get his thoughts out in the open.

"Why would you go to the trouble of toying with my emotions, playing me for a fool, teasing me with your wiles, if all you were interested in was getting your hands on that money?" He rubbed at the back of his neck with one hand. "And then during the drive home, it dawned on me. You were retaliating. You were looking for some kind of revenge because I'd hurt you all those years ago when you left Pine Meadow."

His shoulders squared and he tipped up his chin just enough to give Amber the impression that he was looking down on her.

"Well," he said, "your trip to Pine Meadow has

been a complete success. You've brought me to my knees and you've procured your monetary reward for all the hardship you suffered over the past ten years."

His sarcasm was like a smack in the face.

"What I suggest you do," he said, "is take your money and get the hell out of Pine Meadow. You're not wanted here."

"That's not true!"

Sydney ran from the hallway where she'd obviously been hiding, *and* eavesdropping.

"I want you to be here," Sydney said, her voice bordering on hysteria as she threw her arms around Amber's waist. "I don't want you to go anywhere. I don't care what Dad says. You can't go. You can't!"

Amber's throat constricted. Sydney's overwhelming anxiety made her eyes well, and those tears blurred her vision as she looked over at Jon.

His jaw knotted with emotion, anger at her, concern for their daughter, apprehension for the situation they found themselves in, Amber couldn't tell. All she knew was that she felt very irritated with him for not rushing to comfort Sydney.

"Honey," she crooned, bending over and hugging her daughter tight to her chest, "it's going to be okay." She felt Sydney's body trembling and knew how troubled her daughter was over the prospect of losing her mother just when they'd found each other.

"You promise?" Sydney whispered against Amber's shirt.

"Of course I do," Amber said, leading Sydney out of the room. "Come on. Let me take you to your room. Your dad and I can't talk this out unless you give us a little privacy."

Once they were in Sydney's bedroom, Amber settled her daughter into the desk chair. Then Amber squatted down and gazed into Sydney's young, frightened eyes.

"Honey, this problem is between me and your dad," Amber explained. "It has nothing to do with you."

"But Dad's shouting."

"Well," Amber said, "he's angry. And people sometimes shout when they're angry. But he's not angry with you. And neither am I. We both love you very much." She smoothed her fingertips over Sydney's forearm. "Now I don't want you to worry. We'll work this out."

"He told you to go away."

Amber smiled, and she knew the monumental power of her maternal love for her child shone through her eyes. "Nothing and no one will ever be able to separate us, Sydney. Do you believe me?"

Sydney nodded silently.

"And didn't I already promise that I wouldn't leave town without saying goodbye?"

Again, Sydney nodded.

"I want you to trust me." Amber stood up and planted a gentle kiss on top of her daughter's head. "I also want you to study hard so you can get an A on your spelling test. Just for me."

Amber went to the door.

"Mom?"

She turned back. "Yes, sweetie?" '

"I'll get an A," Sydney whispered. "Just for you." After blowing her daughter a kiss, she closed Sydney's door and made her way back toward the kitchen.

She pondered her next move. She could go back in that room and plead her case; she could tell him her side of the story in the hopes of clearing her name. Or she could let him go on believing whatever awful things his mother had told him.

Of one thing she was completely sure—she was

sick to death of being judged. And it was at that moment, when she stood in the kitchen doorway and Jon's eyes bored into her, that she was struck with a sudden, life-altering realization. One she couldn't possibly keep to herself.

"All those years ago when you and I dated," she began, wanting him to understand the full impact of her revelation when she finally revealed it, "I was made to feel that I wasn't good enough. By your parents. And by you. Everyone was giving me the message that I was unworthy of you."

Jon looked clearly taken aback. "I never felt you weren't good enough. Never."

"Oh, yes, you did." She crossed her arms tightly over her chest. "Otherwise, we wouldn't have had to keep our relationship a secret from your parents."

"We kept our relationship from your father, too," he said pointedly.

"But you know very well that we did that because you were three years older than I was. He would never have allowed his fifteen-year-old daughter to date an eighteen-year-old young man. Would you allow that for Sydney?" Before he had a chance to answer, she raised her brows and said, "If you're entirely truthful here, you'll admit that you didn't want to tell your parents about us because you *knew* they wouldn't approve of me."

He averted his guilty gaze to the floor for a split second and then directed his eyes back to her face.

"With your silence," she continued, "you relayed the clear message to me that you agreed with them."

Jon's tone was low as he said, "You're wrong. I didn't agree with them. That wasn't the message I meant to convey."

"Ah, but to me, the important thing is," she said, "that's the message *I received*. And worse, that's the message *I believed*." Almost to herself, she said, "All my life, I've felt... unworthy. Not good enough."

The ire she'd been holding at bay, burst forth, like water rushing over a dam.

"But walking down that hallway just now," she said, "I was overcome with the most marvelous thought. It doesn't matter what you think of me. It doesn't matter what your mother thinks of me. What matters is what *I* think of me." She leveled her gaze on him. "That's what should have mattered to me all along. If I'd made my own opinion more important than everyone else's, I'd have been so much better off."

Leaning against the kitchen counter, Jon said,

"So let me get this straight. Because my parents made you feel inferior, because you claim that I've made you feel inferior, then you think that makes it okay for you to lie, to cheat, to steal? You still haven't explained that," he said, pointing to the bank papers he'd brought home with him.

"Jon, I have no intention of explaining anything to you."

"You don't have to," he said. "The evidence pretty much speaks for itself."

Amber walked to the table, picked up her purse and slid the long leather strap over one shoulder. "I'm so glad this came to light before anything really developed between us. I'd hate to have to go through life feeling the need to explain myself, feeling beholden and eternally grateful to the man who was supposed to love me for who I am."

"Who you are?" He sounded incredulous. "I'm still trying to figure that out. You said the years that have passed have made a difference in us. I didn't want to believe it, but now I can finally agree. I don't know you."

Amber went to the back door and turned the knob, then turned to face him once again. "I'm sure you don't. But you *do* know your mother."

She glanced at the papers sitting on the tiled

counter, then she looked back at him. "Look into it a little further," she advised, her tone as cool and smooth as polished granite. She wouldn't let Jon, or any other Weston for that matter, ever hurt her again. "Dig a little deeper. You just might learn something important."

With that, she walked out, shutting the door firmly behind her.

* * *

The paperwork was complete. Amber signed the official document that would transfer her father's savings account in Weston Savings and Loan into Sydney's name. Sliding the paper into the manila folder along with the small black bankbook, Amber was relieved to have the matter of the money settled once and for all. The account would serve as the beginnings of a college fund for her daughter. That solution made the most logical sense to Amber.

Dropping into Jon's lap the responsibility for making the transfer was Amber's way of being absolutely sure he'd discover the real truth about the money—and about the past. She planned to slip the manila envelope containing the transfer document and the bankbook into his mailbox on her way out of town.

Amber picked up the white envelope, the goodbye note she'd written to Sydney snug inside. The words had been slow in coming, agonizingly hard to write, as Amber had reflected on the deep, incomparable love she'd discovered over the past few weeks since learning she was a mother.

She hoped Sydney would understand her motives behind leaving Pine Meadow so quickly, too quickly to say goodbye face-to-face. Once she was back in Connecticut, Amber would call her daughter every single day. She'd promised Sydney so in the note.

Pressing the letter to her heart, Amber prayed that Jon would see to it that Sydney received her heartfelt message. Then she slipped the note in the manila envelope with the bank papers, sealed it and wrote Jon's name on the front.

The suitcase latches clicked with a depressing finality as she snapped them closed.

Don't look at this like it's an ending, she told herself. Look at it as a new beginning.

She and Jon were a thing of the past. It was silly of her to have thought otherwise. Her relationship with him had been over years ago. Neither one of them could change that.

But her relationship with Sydney was only just beginning, and that was something to be joyous about.

Picking up her suitcase and the manila envelope, she gave the hotel room one last look, and then stepped out into the crisp fall air.

The leaves on the trees lining the highway were just beginning to turn crimson and burnt orange, and Amber rolled down her car window, hoping the cool autumn air might lift her spirits.

An hour later, she pulled off the road at a rest stop for a bite to eat. It wasn't that she was hungry, really, she simply couldn't bring herself to cross the boundary and leave the state of New Jersey. Maybe after a little fortification, she could tackle the obstacle the state line posed.

After lingering over a second cup of coffee, she decided she'd dawdled long enough. It was time to get back on the road.

Amber hadn't been driving twenty minutes before she noticed car lights flashing in her rearview mirror. For a moment, she thought the police may be signaling her to pull over. But then she saw it wasn't a traffic cruiser but a regular car.

Well, not a regular car. It was a souped-up, canary-yellow roadster, hot on her tail.

Jon had followed her.

Amber glared into the rearview mirror. He'd read the note she'd written to Sydney. Amber just knew it. And he'd chased her down with the intention of changing her plans.

She pulled her car to the shoulder of the road. The roadster pulled over behind her.

From the side mirror on her door, she watched him exit his car and walk toward hers. Lord, he looked so good, she thought. Tall and dark and too damned handsome for words. But then a flaring anger took total control of her emotions. How dare he hunt her down like this?

She threw open her car door, storming to a stand. "Just what do you think you're doing? You read Sydney's letter, didn't you? Well, you can't change my mind. I'm going to Connecticut to sell my father's house and resign from my practice and then I'm coming back to Pine Meadow. I'm going to open up an office in the Bowers. You—or your mother—can't keep me out of Pine Meadow. I'm going to see my daughter *every single day*. And nothing you can do or say will stop me."

Just then the front passenger door of the

roadster opened and Sydney jumped out of the car. She ran around to greet her mother.

"Sydney?"

Jon and Amber grabbed for their daughter at the same time and pulled her to safety on the far side of the parked cars where the grass met the shoulder of the road.

"Honey, that was dangerous," Amber gently admonished, her heart pounding a furious beat.

"You need to watch the traffic." Then Jon asked Sydney, "Are you okay?"

"Sure," Sydney answered with a small shrug. "Gosh, adults are so uptight. I was being careful."

After Amber heaved a sigh of relief, she realized that all the anger in her was gone, and she felt confused. Why would Jon bring Sydney if he meant to argue with her about her plans to return to Pine Meadow? She looked down at Sydney and then up at Jon. "What are you two doing here?"

Sydney quickly piped up, "Dad's sorry he shouted at you last night. He didn't mean all those awful things he said. He told me he wanted to—"

"Hold it!" Jon interrupted the child. "Sydney, I really do appreciate your wanting to help here, but if you don't mind, this is something I need to do on my own."

Amber didn't move. She didn't know what to think, what to say about what was happening. She watched her daughter's big brown eyes roll with drama.

Sydney lifted her shoulders and let them drop. "Sure, Dad," she said. "Whatever you want."

"Thanks." Jon's voice was tinged with a mixture of chagrin and more than a little trepidation.

He waited a moment, and then looked down at Sydney. "Would you mind getting lost?" he asked. "Go get in the car. I'd like a little privacy."

"*Da-ad*, we're parked on the side of the highway," she said. "How much privacy do you think you're gonna get?" After huffing an exasperated sigh, Sydney trudged to the roadster and climbed inside.

Some vibrant, unseen energy hummed between Amber and Jon, along with that ever-present attraction. She hated the fact that he still fascinated her so, even after all they'd been through, even after all the pain she'd suffered.

"I did read the note you dropped off for Sydney," he said.

There was something in his tone that made her pulse quicken with some mysterious emotion. Hope? Anticipation?

Don't be silly, she told herself.

"I came home to pick her up after school," he told her, "and I found the envelope you left."

He paused, and time ticked slowly by. Amber moistened her lips. Feeling the need to fill up the silence, she said, "When I realized it was you following me, I assumed you were chasing me down to talk me out of coming back to Pine Meadow."

"No." He shook his head. "That's not why I came."

"Sydney said you came to apologize for shouting at me last night," she said. "You didn't need to drive to the state line for that." Her tone lowered an octave. "Especially when you knew I was coming back. What you had to say could have waited."

"No," he repeated, this time more emphatically, "it couldn't wait."

"Oh."

They looked at each other.

"Amber," he finally said, "I've been such an idiot. I don't know if you can ever forgive me, but I hope you'll try."

Her heartbeat stuttered, but she refused to assume that his apology was anything more than that. A simple apology.

Offering him a small smile, she said, "You're forgiven. We need to get along, you and I. We have a daughter that needs raising."

His groan disclosed real agony. "Please don't tell me that Sydney is the only reason you think we need to get along."

Giddiness jittered in her stomach. But still she felt the need to play it cool.

"Since you came back to town—" Jon stepped closer to her, cupped her elbows in the palms of his hands "—I've had a small taste of what life might have been like for us if all that rotten stuff hadn't happened. If our parents hadn't pulled us apart."

He gazed into her eyes. "I know all about it. My mother was in tears when I finally forced all the details out of her."

"Oh, Jon, I'm sorry." The words were out of Amber's mouth before she could think. "I wanted to tell you. I knew I was going to have to. Especially when we grew closer with each passing day. But I didn't want you to be hurt. And you would have been when you discovered what your mother, our parents, had done, and—" she paused "—I didn't want you to think badly of my father."

Her explanation seemed jumbled, confused, but

from the look on his face, she could tell he understood.

"Unfortunately I do realize that everyone concerned, your dad, my parents, were doing what they thought was best for us." He sighed. "There's simply no excuse for my mother's actions, ten years ago or a few days ago. But the fact that your father could never bring himself to spend the money has to say something in his favor, don't you think?"

"Yeah, I guess." Amber looked down at the ground. "But I've missed so much, Jon. So much of Sydney's life."

"It breaks my heart to think about that," he said softly. "I'm so sorry you were lied to. Hell, I'm sorry *I* was lied to." He squeezed her arms just enough to get her to look into his eyes. "I'm sorry I didn't believe you when you said you'd been told that Sydney hadn't survived. But most of all..."

The intensity in his gaze had Amber mesmerized. "I'm sorry that I didn't believe *in* you when my mother was maligning your character yet again just yesterday. You were so right. I do know her. I know what kind of person she is. I should have known better than to listen to her."

After a moment, Amber couldn't help but remark "The world just seems to be against us."

"Oh, no," he said. "Not the whole world. That little girl back there, she's for us. One hundred percent."

A smile curled Amber's lips. "She's a sweetheart."

"She loves you," Jon said. Then he added, "I love you."

Her breath caught in her throat. Had he really spoken those three little words?

Somehow she found herself in his arms, hugging him like there was no tomorrow.

"I couldn't let you go off without telling you," he whispered against her ear.

"Oh, Jon," she said, tears of joy flowing, emotion lumping in her throat, "I love you. I've always loved you. I don't think I ever stopped."

He kissed her then, right there on the side of the highway, his mouth desperate and hungry.

"If you guys can quit being mushy for a minute," Sydney called from the car window, "I have something I want to tell Mom."

"Can't it wait?" Jon growled good-naturedly. "I'm busy here."

Amber chuckled. "What is it, honey?" she asked Sydney.

"I got an A on my spelling test."

"Wow! That's great," Amber said.

"Life is great!" Jon shouted for all the world to hear, and he picked up Amber and whirled her around in a circle.

Throwing her head back, Amber laughed with abandon. And she knew with no uncertainty that her small family would beat all the odds fate or the world could throw at them. All the wrongs of the past had been righted, all the secrets revealed. The happiness she had found with Jon and Sydney was more than enough to last a lifetime.

* * *

Thank you for taking the time to read Made in Paradise. If you enjoyed the book, please tell a friend about it or consider writing a review. Word-of-mouth recommendations and good reviews are the best advertising tool an author can have. Thank you very much for your help and support. On the following pages, you'll find a note from Donna, a list of her other titles, and her bio.

A Note From the Author

I love it when two people are brought together by a vulnerable child and they end up falling madly in love. I have used the theme in other books and I've tied them together in a sweet romance series called A Family Forever. I hope you'll look for other books in the series.

Let's keep in touch. Please consider joining my mailing list so you will be alerted to new releases, sale promotions, favorite recipes, giveaways, and more. I will never share your email address. You can find my blog here.

All my love,
Donna Fasano

Other Books by Donna Fasano

Ocean City Boardwalk Series:
Following His Heart, Book 1
Two Hearts In Winter, Book 2
Wild Hearts of Summer, Book 3
An Almost Perfect Christmas, Book 4
Grown-Up Christmas List, Book 5
The Wedding Planner's Son, Book 6

~ ~ ~

Reclaim My Heart
The Merry-Go-Round
Her Fake Romance
Take Me, I'm Yours
His Wife for a While
An Accidental Family
Mountain Laurel

~ ~ ~

The Single Daddy Club Series:

Other Books by Donna Fasano

Derrick, Book 1
Jason, Book 2
Reece, Book 3

~ ~ ~

A Family Forever Series:
A Beautiful Stranger, Book 1
Made in Paradise, Book 2
and others

~ ~ ~

Non-fiction Books
Cooking In All Directions
Prayer of Quiet
Favorite Christmas Cookies
Recipes of Love
Guy Food

About the Author

Donna Fasano is a USA TODAY Bestselling Author whose books have sold nearly 4 million copies worldwide and have been translated into two dozen languages. She lives on Maryland's Eastern Shore with her husband Bill and Roo, their thirteen-year-old Australian cattle dog mix.

www.ingramcontent.com/pod-product-compliance
Lightning Source LLC
Chambersburg PA
CBHW050023180626
46810CB00002B/546